T0087915

INTIMACY

A NOVEL

INTIMACY

A NOVEL

S<small>TANLEY</small> C<small>RAWFORD</small>

TUSCALOOSA

Copyright © 2016 by Stanley Crawford
The University of Alabama Press
Tuscaloosa, Alabama 35487-0380
All rights reserved
Manufactured in the United States of America

FC2 is an imprint of The University of Alabama Press

Inquiries about reproducing material from this work should be addressed to
the University of Alabama Press

Book Design: Publications Unit, Department of English, Illinois State
Univeristy, Director: Steve Halle, Production Assistant: Tess Culton
Cover Design: Lou Robinson
Typeface: Garamond

⊗

The paper on which this book is printed meets the minimum requirements
of American National Standard for Information Sciences—Permanence of
Paper for Printed Library Materials, ANSI Z39.48–1984

Library of Congress Cataloging-in-Publication Data

Names: Crawford, Stanley G., 1937- author.
Title: Intimacy : a novel / Stanley Crawford.
Description: Tuscaloosa, Alabama : FC2 is an imprint of The University of
   Alabama Press, [2016] | Description based on print version record and
CIP
   data provided by publisher; resource not viewed.
Identifiers: LCCN 2015044321 (print) | LCCN 2015040882 (ebook) |
ISBN
   9781573668590 (eBook) | ISBN 9781573660549 (pbk. : alk. paper)
Subjects: LCSH: Psychological fiction.
Classification: LCC PS3553.R295 (print) | LCC PS3553.R295 I58 2016
(ebook) |
   DDC 813/.54--dc23
LC record available at http://lccn.loc.gov/2015044321

for Ken Baumann

INTIMACY

"For whom left am I first…?"
—Lucie Brock-Broido

The surf was running high, to judge from the delicate rattling of the loose pane in the bathroom window that I could sometimes hear prolonging itself an instant after the strongest reverberations. A wind had come up. Through the half-closed curtains, the plate-glass windows of the living room were smeared with salt-spray. A few evening strollers bundled up in layers of fleece paced along the sea walk, a short section of which was visible through my northwest window, where I had not fully closed the drapes. Toward this vertical slash of waning light my eyes were again and again drawn as I paced, and sat, and stood, and paced again.

It began with my right running shoe, an old one I had been many months intending to throw out but kept hanging on to for a last wear or two—this pair I bought perhaps two or three years ago and which I used for rough or dirty walks—such as I might have taken today, with the surf high and messy, or when it rained, as it could again soon for that matter, and which I wore to work this morning knowing that nobody would notice them beneath the skirting of the desk. And it was Friday: the scuffed footwear announced an intention to head for desert or mountain or to another beach without delay at the end of the workday. The lace would soon go, I suspected, so I was careful even when untying and unloosening it, while preparing to slip my socked foot out of its confinement.

Laces loosened, I paused. I had carefully planned this moment. Or not carefully so much as obsessively: I did not occupy myself with the actual details of it. These I already knew—from before. It was almost seven. I had just returned home from work. I knew what I was beginning again. I had considered this action for over a year, perhaps even for years, it may even have been a germ that lay quietly within a series of gestures that had always until now ended in my standing in a darkened room alone late in the evening or in the early hours of the morning, even at dawn, on the way to the shower or to bed, a man momentarily aware of the cool waxed floor under his bare soles and of faint breezes ventilating moist areas of bare skin. I paused in untying or rather loosening my right shoe, noting the smudges of green on its dirty white or once-white leather and rubber, and wondering whether I really wanted to embark on this again—or if in fact I would be able to go through with it to completion at last.

The running shoes—it came back to me—had been purchased at a flea market from a cadaverously thin man with dark skin and an oiled brush of black hair, a long curl of which sprung out over the center of his forehead and touched the bridge of his nose. He wore a gold ring on each of his finely sculpted hands. The shoes, probably hijacked, were half retail price. Even as he counted out the change and lay it into my palm I could feel his slightly crossed eyes drawing new customers to his stall. "Good shoes. Best brands." Then rattling off the names. "Only best brands."

But a plan—no. More a matter of having decided that at a certain moment I would pull down a barrier within and step over to the other side in order to see what was there. Any delays beyond a certain point might release the poisons of doubt—or of yet more doubt.

Such was the argument that convinced me to take off my right shoe. I was sitting on the edge of the unmade bed gripping the sole with my left hand, sensing the contours of its tracings of the human foot, which momentarily seemed odd. My feet have never given me the slightest trouble. The house creaked—as it often did when the surf was high. With a flip, I tossed the running shoe toward the closet. It tumbled through the open doorway with a hollow bang and then a subsiding shuffle, leaving a trail of rubbery scent. My clothes—the rest of my clothes beside what I had on and what was stuffed into a white cotton laundry bag leaning into the right corner of the closet, plus a clump of underwear on the floor next to the toilet, and then my recent load of clean laundry dumped in a jumble in a dresser drawer—my shirts and jeans and coats hung from the closet rod in a neat file of blues and grays and blacks as if standing in some secret line whose existence the sliding open of the door had surprised.

O

The lace was already loose in my left shoe. I had noted this while leaving the office, but compelled by the almost sexual urgency that had overcome me to be back home to begin on this thing, I had left it loose though had made a mental note to be careful getting out of the car and back inside on what turned out to be an impulsive stop on the way home, and keep an eye on it while climbing the redwood steps to the back door in the foggy dimness of what passes for dusk this time of year. I remembered. I didn't trip. I nursed the loosening shoelace, foot slightly arched to hold the shoe on, while I peeled and ate an orange at the kitchen sink and stared out across the living room through the spray-misted triangular window in the shape of a sail that looks out over the fences and sundecks of three beach houses to the south and where, weekday evenings, I could watch the dim motions of what I took to be a man in the second house showering his chest and arms punctually at six-fifteen—when I was home at that hour—and blurrily washing his hair more or less every other of those days. Weekends he did not shower, at least at a regular hour. This evening, the upstairs window was dark. I threw the peels down the garbage disposal and washed my hands.

The shoe stayed on, if barely, as I limped across the living room to the bedroom and sat down on the bed and, habit overriding the emergency, took off the other one first. The left of course did not need untying: a matter of lifting the foot out of the shoe, whose heel I held down with my socked foot. The shoe came off with the ease of a slipper—though I have not worn slippers in years. I bent over and picked it up and turned it over and examined its worn tread of rows of fine chevrons incised in the gray rubber, in which grains of sand were embedded even though three days had passed since my last walk on the beach. I pried some of these out with fingernails, in one of those quiet instants when the surf suddenly goes calm, and I heard the grains bounce on the bare hardwood floor with tiny pricks of sound like bubbles popping.

A delaying tactic to be sure. I had no curiosity or interest in observing the gritty minutiae of the moment in and of themselves—so much as to flush out the definitive hesitation, the doubt, that might instead convince me to do what I usually did—to change my clothes, run back down the stairs and climb into my car, check my cell phone, which I never bring up to the apartment, and drive out into the night.

I remembered then what I already knew but which in my excitement I persisted in forgetting—that this was Friday evening and that I was therefore not due back at work until Monday morning at nine.

Somehow that decided it. Perhaps there was no logic in most decisions, only the semblance. I turned over the shoe and tossed it into the closet where it spun around like a bowling pin and settled upside down in a corner far from its mate.

○

I neglected to consider my jacket, which I had worn defiantly to work in place of the regulation sports coat, as if to say along with the running shoes that I was going to have a long pleasurable weekend with no time to waste getting ready for it after work, that I was going to launch myself straight into it. I had sloughed the jacket off the minute I stepped inside the back door and had draped it over the back of a kitchen chair—an artificially faded denim item with collar and angled pocket flaps of cherry red corduroy recently ordered online and charged to a vague future, though a glitch on the web site necessitated a conversation with a courteous woman's voice against a background hiss of static. I remember suppressing an urge to ask where she was, probably some tech center on the Indian sub-continent. Which thoughts settled over me as I sat on the edge of the bed staring down at my socks.

I stood. Normally as a matter of course I do not stand in order to take off my socks, though I have been known to do so, but in this instance it was not my socks, or thought of my socks, a dazzlingly white woolly blend of cotton and polyester that I had bought only two weeks before in a bulk packet on sale—that drew me to my feet: it was my ring, and therefore my watch as well, because these also I most often put on and take off together, almost as one gesture, usually watch first, in putting it on, for the simple reason that it is what I first see and lay my hand on; and ring second, because it so often becomes pushed under something else on top of the chest of drawers, a handkerchief, my wallet, scraps of paper, or even in the gap under the porcelain lamp base that its residual or incipient feet, squarish nubbin-like things, create between the base and the glass surface of the chest of drawers. I am always lifting the lamp to see what has slipped under there. It came with the place, as did the chest of drawers.

I have no fixed routine about ring and watch. Sometimes I come into the apartment and walk straight through the kitchen and living room, actually living-dining room, into the bedroom and slip off ring and watch first thing, while at other times I'll keep them on for several minutes—sorting through the mail—or often wandering over to the wicker armchair and settling myself down into it to a crescendo of creaks, drapery open to the last shafts of sunlight of the afternoon or early evening, and sit there as if a visitor to my own house and life, ring still on right little finger, watch still upon left wrist. Of course I have also been known to come home only for a moment, to pick up something I left behind or for a snack or even a short rest before resuming my errand or before heeding whatever is calling me back outside, even a walk or run on the beach; but the main point is that as long as I keep watch and ring on inside the apartment it means—to me—that I am only provisionally or temporarily here. Taking them off with little flourishes is sign that I am at home, at least for an hour or two.

The confusion that raised me to my stockinged feet lay precisely in this: why of all days when I knew I had committed myself to staying within these walls for an extended period of time did I fail to walk straight to the bedroom and slip off my ring and watch? Even going so far as to peel and eat an orange with ring and watch dancing right in front of my face, those quietly glittering presences that highlight my quotidian dexterities. So I stood for a moment in the dim light of the bedroom and pondered this, left index finger and thumb twisting the ring around and around on my right little finger before slipping it off—knowing that I would slip it off in an instant, as soon as I had figured out why I had failed to do so fifteen minutes before.

I have been told that I have fine hands. In any case the fingers are long for my height, with narrow high domed nails, almost feminine, and an even sprinkling of short dark hairs that creeps out from the wrist and which tapers down toward the knuckle of the little finger of each hand, as if worn away, with thin little forests of curved hairs on the first and second segments of each finger and thumb. I apparently have a habit of readily displaying them and letting them linger on countertops and desktops, so as to prolong conversations of a casual or trivial nature—mannerism I was unaware of for years until on three occasions in a single day, within hours of each other, my ring was commented on, causing me to become attentive to an aspect of my behavior I had taken for granted. There is nothing particularly extraordinary about the ring: simple gold band inlaid with irregular chips of aquamarine and other greenish and bluish gemstones whose names I no longer remember—in a pattern, if you can call it that, which resembles in miniature the irregular lines and shapes of a flagstone path. Like all rings, it is, I suppose, a kind of talisman to protect me, to guard who I am—that is, when I am outside, a-swim in the world, walking on the beach or driving the car or in a crowd somewhere, a movie theater, shopping mall, bar, restaurant, places like that. Inside, indoors, at home, I have a surfeit of such reminders, even though I constantly cull them down to what I think of as a bare minimum, which is why I take it off—or indeed why I release myself from its constraints in this space where by contrast I would more often wish to be other than what I am—this walled space, these rooms, where I am more likely than in any other place to make the leap to become an entirely other being. So off came the ring. A cheerful tinkling sound announced that it left the grip of my left thumb and index finger and reached the refuge of the perfectly flat inertness of the plate glass top of the chest of drawers.

I mean of course: habitually. At the moment in question I had not yet finished twirling it around on my little finger, its perch for twelve to sixteen hours a day. A ring is also a link to another person or even a group, I suppose, and though I had come to think of this one as disconnected from any other person, I also knew that in some sense it was a mooring point for another life—or so it would be commonly read by other people who looked down at my hands and whose attention would be then caught by the ring, and that they would imagine filaments leading off invisibly toward another person, a lover, a companion, whatever: which oddly I took had come to read in the gleam of the gold band, that there was or would soon be somebody else to which it connected—even while knowing how unlikely that had become—and which I knew even then, at that moment I bought it four years before, alone, for no one else but myself, under the canvas awning of a booth at a mountain resort, late in an afternoon, in the bright orange light of the cloud-furled sun. The jewelry maker with dark pupil-less eyes and straight black hair spoke with a melodious voice: "It shows off your hands marvelously." A wild thought, which I did not voice, darted through my mind: Then I could protect myself from meddlesome queries and long conversations. Instead, I laughed aloud. And when I complained—to myself, really—about the expense, she chimed back, "You deserve it."

I slipped it off. I was able to slip it off because at last I had worked out that since I had come home in an over-excited mood it was as if I was not coming home at all, but was only coming home to rush out again into the night, toward those glinting moments I knew I could imagine and yet could never discover—and would, did I dare look far enough into the future, finally return home weary and dispirited again, the breath of others clinging to my clothes and hair, as always—forgetting as I so often do that the trick is never to look too far ahead or, for that matter, too far back.

O

I almost forgot the watch. These things usually go together, but not always. I was halfway back to the bed when I remembered. I stepped back to the chest of drawers. I was, I decided, in two places at once, living two lives at once, the one I thought I was aware of—at, to look down at the brushed gold face of the watch, seven-sixteen pm—plus another that I had not yet managed to dredge up into full consciousness but which pulled at me as if from several or even many time zones away: like a day that you have meticulously planned for weeks in advance and in which you have invested a full complement of fear and anticipation, of worry and delight, only to discover at the last minute that everything has been cancelled—leaving you to live through the actual day, when it finally arrives, in some habitual pattern while you imagination runs free and reconstructs the lost moments one by one, the things you would be doing now, in that place, in this time, with this or that person, the fantasy day of the child who is told that the trip to the zoo is off, the picnic in the mountains, the ride in the special train down the coast—in that childhood buried within the casing of the adult, where it lies shrunken and desiccated, lifeless, resisting the digestion of forgetfulness.

But I had it backwards: this was the unusual day, starting now, starting from the moment I had entered the house or had tossed my cell phone on the car seat and closed and locked the car door behind me, and what I was leaving behind or living on top of, in an archeological sense, was my ordinary day—and you could say that it was what I was in fact already beginning to miss but had not yet managed to take into account: it was the ordinary day I was leaving behind in order to embark on the singular—on that which, at last, would never repeat itself.

But I was also aware, looking down on the round face of the watch, how likely that this day was to come to a weary and confused end just like all the others that had led up to it—though I am careful never to convey the impression that such is how I end any of my days. I had not removed the watch from my wrist, I had merely spread my fingers under its metal expansion band to stretch the spring-loaded links enough to slip it over my hand, where I now flexed them. I have been told that there is something about my trim and wiry build, even my relative shortness, that conveys the impression that I know exactly where I am going in both a minute-by-minute sense and in a larger philosophical way and that even conveys the certainty that I am almost there. This very moment my fellow workers, if they bothered, would imagine me racing over the mountain pass or checking into a hotel on a cliff overlooking the protected coves. Large awkward people fed too much protein and fat in their youths either instinctively fear me, if I read their gestures correctly, or wish to clasp me in their fleshy arms—I am too firm, too precise, too proportioned for them to leave me untouched, ungrasped. I have learned to protect myself. I lower my tall bulbous forehead—but I caricature myself, it is not all that tall or bulbous—and glower a little. "You look like a dolphin when you do that," someone once said to me, "an unsmiling dolphin." Which leads to a thought that has often come to me, that yes, outwardly I appear to be determinedly, purposefully, charting a course, to others that watch me pass, while to my eyes beneath the surface, in the murkiness, all directions appear the same.

I slipped the watch over my hand and laid it with a splashing metallic sound on the glass next to the ring—which skidded out of sight under the lamp base.

○

But I always miss my watch at first—the unthinking conve-
nience of being able to glance down with a slight left turn of
the head and eyes at the perpetually changing angles of the three
hands—though also, and this is what finally carries the most
weight, there comes the relief of not having to do so, to look
down, the relief of being free of the watch face that always after
a time becomes too familiar. I seek a factual detail from it: the
time. But also I seek the reassurance that comes from a carefully
crafted—or manufactured—object that is both familiar and mysterious. So when I am free of it, leaving it on the chest of drawers
or on the wicker arm of the sofa, I must also resume the faint labor of imagining or remembering or estimating the time—from
which I eventually will seek an equally faint rest by putting on
my watch again. I have no other working clock in the apartment.

But at this particular moment, even in the dim light, I
noticed what I rarely do otherwise, the indentations and pinch
marks of the expansion band on my wrist—and then, as I moved
in stocking feet over to the doorway where there was more light
from the living room windows, that place where over these past
months the watch had shadowed the skin from the sun, creating
atop my wrist a white disk. And then, drawing closed to a floor
lamp in the living room, the one I leave on all the time day and
night, I could make out the thin whitish band on my right little
finger where my ring had also prevented the skin from darkening.

I tan quickly and dark, even swarthy, which gives the
untanned areas of my body a bright luminosity, such as under my

arms, my buttocks, and where the straps of thongs cross my feet. When untanned I can be as pale as anyone, and I take particular pleasure in those gradations of tone from the fully darkened to the shadowy, lighter areas of the body, though this particular evening I did not know how to regard the half-dollar size disk atop my wrist—was this a blemish or was it somehow one of those irregularities that could also be considered attractive? And thus would I be inclined to look at it—as now, suddenly conscious of it—with considerable frequency throughout the course of the evening? And would it then have some peculiar distortion on the unfolding of the hours I would be passing here, perhaps because I had not taken sufficiently into account the effects of these shadowings, these marks of clothing projected upon my body?

The rows of indentations and pinch marks would soon fade, I knew—and indeed virtually had by the time I glanced a second time at my slightly veined and tendoned wrist as, reaching, it pulled free of the cuff.

○

But my car is a kind of clothing—thought which was teasing at my consciousness either on my way to work that morning or returning home in the evening, I was not certain which: a kind of autonomous clothing that swallows up its wearer. It is what I put on and take off two and three and four times a day, as I slip in and out of it in the garage downstairs, and in the dark, crowded parking lots—this padded wheeled shell I wrap around myself. The salesman almost said as much. The car was the sportiest version of a new line with a made-up name. "Is this the car you really want to be?"—question I at first drew back from, as crossing a line the situation did not call for, or so at least I feigned. The salesman was tall and lanky, of almost albino paleness, who chewed gum and jangled keys, and too young for a shiny grey suit. He couldn't make up his mind whether to call me by my first or last name and kept trying out versions to see what would most please me, placing misters before first, last, first and last, then leaving it off altogether. A framed family photograph in color, himself, a young wife, three blond toddlers, stared down on us from a shelf behind his desk in the cramped cubicle, but I had the peculiar feeling it was a posed photograph of a borrowed family. He wore no wedding ring, only a heavy high school class ring with a bright blue synthetic stone.

That was a year ago. Driving often gives me an erection, especially when I am setting out at night or on a sunny weekend afternoon toward some imagined adventure, and I accept once again the hope of the daringly sculpted and padded interior and lean into the fluid movement of the street and then the highway, and I can drive for hours in any direction, in the solitude of schools of metal fishes, in a trance of prolonged expectation— even hundreds of miles, even to the end of the day, until I finally pull up exhausted to a motel with a bright orange sign and its offer of anonymous sleep and forgetfulness.

But clothing, yes. I always know where the car is, how far away, like a jacket or sweat shirt, and remember the gestures by which I stepped out of it, and anticipated those that will carry me back inside it. I casually watch it and keep tabs on it and imagine it throughout the day and night.

I knew this very moment without having to think about it that the car lay directly below my bedroom, that it sat in the garage silently, its metal having ceased ticking an hour ago, that it was now silent and cool except perhaps the center of its long gray hood, which might still be warm to the touch.

○

Actually these were not the socks I got on sale, I realized as I drove my right thumb down into my right sock, leg lifted, left hand grasping the jamb or the doorway between the bedroom and the living room for support. Unlike those, these had a band of blue woven into the elastic. I wondered why I persisted in remembering these details weeks or even months afterward, except that there always seems to be something haunting in these visits—in this case to a sporting goods store where I ended up buying a half-dozen pair of socks from a dispirited sales clerk— one of those young men whose face I could no longer remember who seek such jobs in the hope of being close to a source of fitness—but who discover after a short time that these places are sinks of stagnant light and air where nothing more energetic takes place than the lifting of wallets and small parcels. Ten minutes is all I can tolerate: after that I begin to hear the buzzing of the lights and the hum of motors through thin partitions and I begin to smell the poisonous odors of off-gassing synthetics, and I leave.

The sock came off easily enough. I was roughly equidistant between the laundry bag in the bedroom closet and the pile of dirty underwear on the floor next to the toilet but I was in no mood to do the efficient, tidy thing, which would have been to walk over and combine the one dirty and still warm sock with the clump of underwear on the floor and stuff the whole into the bag—because of the still uncertain status of the one newly removed sock, which dangled from my right hand. I had put it on fresh only this morning and thus felt it still had some wear left in it under normal circumstances, but this led to the question of how and when I might be wanting to put it on again, in how many hours or for that matter in how many days, if ever again. The tidy and efficient thing, adding to the laundry bag, implied the resumption of what I thought of as normal life within some reasonable amount of time—generally I do my laundry on Wednesday evenings—while the point of taking off this particular sock lay in the thought that none of this might ever be the same again.

○

That is why I let it slip from my fingers and drop to the hardwood floor in a place where, unless I kicked or brushed it aside, it would prevent the door from fully closing. And where it would rest throughout the night perhaps as a reminder of how the night was to be different from all that had led to it and all, presumably, that would flow from it. I noted at that instant the narrow band of cream wall paint that, because of poor masking, overlapped on to the honey-colored oak flooring. Then I put my right foot down and pressed it against the cool wood surface and felt the air circulate through the heat-damp interstices of my toes, and curl around those particularly sensitive areas, the hollows between heel and ankle bone.

Two thoughts approached from opposite directions: one, what if despite everything, the night turned out to be not at all unusual but quite ordinary instead, other than that I had tried yet one more time through these bizarre means, or means that would seem bizarre to others, to force some equally obscure issue? But that of course is always the risk or indeed even the likelihood— that in fact I would go through with it all and find absolutely nothing had changed, and that I would be left with nothing more than the bland recollection of yet another night spent in a darkened apartment—another night like thousands before it, or rather like those others, which I could not count, in which I had traced these same steps into the late hours, always to the same edge.

The point, or a new view of it, may have been what came to me at the same time as this familiar doubt, with its steady contempt. But then it slipped away in the confusion of the moment. I was left with nothing more than the thought, which for an instant had an odd irrelevancy to it, that I should take off the other sock.

I did so, letting it too fall where I stood. As I turned then to face the living room, I lifted one bare foot and then the other. Over the distant muffled surf I could hear the sound of my soles, momentarily sticky with perspiration, peeling themselves away from the waxed floor.

The loss of this other thought paralyzed me for a time toward the center of the living room where my bare feet had sought the refuge of an island of throw rug, a thickly woven rectangle of gray and black wool. A tentative gust of wind pushed at the building. A neighbor's awning pole banged. Were they home tonight? Would they go out on their deck and tie a bungee cord or length of twine around the pole—or would they be back late, this being Friday night? They? They—or he or she—lived in an apartment across the alley, just north of mine; I had so rarely seen them out on their deck that they could easily have been a succession of tenants, not the same ones, who had each learned how to deal with a noisy awning pole by tying it tight against the railing.

The other thought re-formed, or perhaps it was an echo of it distorted by the distance it had traveled, as it came back not quite new and even a little fragmented, to the effect that whatever I did or did not do as a person, as a sentient being, I did not matter, and that my presence and actions were no more significant in the world than the wear I put on the tires of my car or the marks I may accidentally place on these walls. I have learned of course never to give voice to such thoughts. But this was the view I habitually and even at times cheerfully embraced: that I was nothing, a mote, a speck, a grain of sand—and so, I suppose, my attentiveness to whatever is at the edge of what

I must otherwise perceive, those motes, those grains of sand, the films of moisture, those faintest of breezes, those magnetic impulses inside the plastic cases, and other disturbances created by the armies of nameless helots who skim along the electronic rivers, among them myself, and the flickering touch of whose countless fingers serve to nudge the vast digital glacier down the slope toward who knows what.

And therefore if I am nothing—and if therefore I wish to waste no time making some futile mark on the smooth white plaster of the wall—which will be erased or painted over or defaced or will vanish in collapse—then what choice is there but to become even more so? Perhaps it comes down to something like this: that while most of my species will seek to inflate themselves into something so large as to create the illusion of permanence in the face of eternity, I seek the opposite, to diminish and reduce and shrink myself down to something that will slip from the world without anyone noticing—not even, perhaps, that thing I once considered to be myself—in that last flickering instant of afterthought.

○

So then—I told myself—proceed. But I was by now far ahead. I had reached that moment when I was beginning to loosen my belt. I was still standing on the throw rug when I slowly slipped my belt from the pants loops in the usual clockwise direction, one loop at a time until halfway around, when I was able to pull it free the rest of the way by the buckle. The belt, a dark blue woven cloth affair with a matte black metal buckle which gripped the material with rows of teeth, I had bought a month or so ago at one of those so-called surplus stores that sell clothing and odds and ends to those seeking the paramilitary look—but I was so uncomfortable at the macho grimness of the place, where I had been drawn to a too-innocent curiosity, and whose displays perhaps represented the stunted vision of the close-cropped, tatooed smoker who wordlessly punched the price into an old mechanical cash register, that I nearly walked out without buying the utilitarian belt. 'Webbed' is the term I was searching for, to describe the material. I retraced my steps to the bedroom and hung the belt on a hook inside the door.

I did not as a matter of course take off the belt every time I took off my pants, only when the latter needed washing, as was the case this evening—or would need washing next Wednesday, or eventually. I had worn them only this one day for wet and messy weather and they were splashed around the calves with stains of muddy water kicked up by my heels, from those short distances across parking lots I had to walk or—this morning—run. Beltless, the jeans rode loosely on my hips as I slipped my wallet and comb from right rear pocket and then keys, pen knife from right front pocket, and money clip and bills (which had slipped out of its grasp) and handkerchief from left front, tossing and dump all on the glass top of the chest of drawers, just inside the door, in a succession of quick gestures that had always been automatic—and remained so even when the need for them being automatic was fading away.

I had gone to the bank that afternoon, a Friday, during my lunch hour, as I usually do, but so far had spent none of the cash I had folded into my money clip, an amount not worth worrying about—or so reason told me; and in fact I never carry large amounts of cash, not out of a fear of being mugged, supposing there is an element of rationality in who is mugged and who is not. Appearances, not what one hides, must trigger the stalking urge—and perhaps I come across as an average well-heeled person, even if the contents of my money clip would state quite clearly that I keep cash on hand deliberately low—to the point that the bank tellers must wonder why I stand in line instead of using the machines in the foyer or the parking lot or the drive-up window for such paltry amounts drawn on such a healthy bank balance.

Of course they did not know that I stood in line and presented my check and counted my change and slipped the bills between the gold jaws of the clip in order to study the strangeness of the situation: the concentrated earnestness with which the tellers meticulously keep track of this numerical projection of my person, abstract yet intimate at the same time, within a space that is both so public and so private at the same time (something of which public restrooms also convey) and where nakedness consists of banknotes being displayed too long or in too great quantities—and where while the teller and I stand face to face, though to be more exact the teller sits on a raised chair on her side of the counter, like a prisoner and visitor, within each arms reach of each other, yet in a situation where it is agreed that we are never to touch—and where, as a customer or account-holder or whatever I am called, I can know the luxury of being able to stare at the bare arms and throat and face and hair of a woman who must remain so absorbed in counting and registering that she will be unable to repel my gaze except with a quick sidelong glance and polite unfocused smile—even the one usually on the far right who once, but only once, called me by name; but who then, as if violating some rule of the place, retreated to the safer "Thank you" and "Have a nice day" accompanied by the dull flash of a mechanical smile.

This is what spiraled through my mind as I leaned over the chest of drawers and slid the irregular Z of bills back into the unadorned gold money clip from which they had slipped, these being the new but now folded bills I had requested of the teller—while refraining from adding the possible "as usual" that might have been construed as an invitation to chat. Her arms and their fine blonde hairs were half covered with loose silky sleeves of dark green, and a heavy bracelet of gold links weighed on her thin wrist. I could think of nothing bright to say.

And in removing the bills from my pockets—but not the coins, which I had dumped into the center console of the car— I realized that this was a qualitatively different act than taking off my jacket or socks: here I was removing myself from not something I could be said to own or possess in the way I own my own clothes and furniture and car, but some kind of bridging object that linked me—because it was the substance of exchange, not possession—to an infinite number of people—or, if not quite infinite, to an almost infinite number of possible transactions. These were tokens, passes. I would hand them in, get them back, ad infinitum, through the course of my life; hence their meticulous likeness, except in matters of wear, to all others of their kind—while the thought of their instability momentarily jarred me and led to a flickering urge to carry them out of the apartment, to hide them away by locking them up in the car or even burying them in the sand on the beach—urge which I quickly dismissed.

They were not objects I could in any sense rationally ponder—but then, was there anything that you held under your gaze too long that would not simply disintegrate into explosions of possibility? The essential risk in short of what I was about, a risk that would be equivalent in some sense to that which would accompany my leaning forward against the synthetic marble of the teller's counter and beginning to ask her questions that had to do with the length of her sleeves and where she had bought the gold bracelet or the small child-like gold rings she wore on her right little finger—or the gold pendant—a tiny bell?—she wore around her neck or the star-shaped earrings—until, as a leaned over farther and farther, to the point that out of the corner of my eye I could see and perhaps even read the small grey screen upon which scrolled, glowing, the numbers of my most private secret, some would say, which is my bank account—and a buzzer would suddenly sound loudly throughout the hushed carpeted room and all eyes would turn in our direction—including those of the armed guard who stood drowsily next to the glass doors.

○

There are five keys on the ring: two brass apartment keys, one steel car key with a black rubberized end and four-button remote, another brass key that fits a lock at work, a storage locker padlock key, also brass, and a flat steel key to my safe-deposit vault at the bank. The one thing I always do but did not this evening was to transfer the keys from the pocket of whatever pair of pants I was taking off, usually jeans, to the pocket of whatever I was going to put on, often other jeans or shorts. The keys' leaning, splayed posture on the glass top of the chest of drawers, like a bird that has fallen to the ground and lies there with ruffled feathers was therefore unusual. I wondered whether they would nag at me throughout the rest of the night for not being tucked away in some pocket in anticipation of the moment I would again step out the door.

I rarely use the front door—it faces in the direction of the beach and opens out onto a narrow porch-balcony and wooden stairs down to a cement walkway normally made impassible, or difficult to traverse, from foot-deep sand-drifts. The heavy wooden frame of the curtained glass door shrinks and swells, binding in unpredictable ways; and I prefer to go out the back door and down the steps along the south side of the garage and out on to the alley that passes for the neighborhood street, to the east-west walkway that leads to the sea walk and to the beach— on those days or evenings I go for walks or runs. The garage and therefore the car are also out the back door, down the steps, but I leave the garage door open and unlocked, having lost the key, and given the fact that I keep nothing of value in that echoing space, though I always lock the car, which sets the alarm, whose only key fits both door and ignition or steering locks. A spare car door key—it has no electronic chip to activate the ignition—is hidden somewhere under the car, in the left rear wheel well, if I remember correctly, in a magnetic case.

Of the other keys, safe deposit box (it opens one of the two locks, the bank holding the key to the other lock), and the key to the padlock of the small storage stall I rent a few miles away, and the key which unlocks the rarely visited paper files at work—none of these do I use on a regular basis. And of course all these keys are standard shapes and sizes, easily duplicated, and their locks doubtless easily picked or forced or drilled out, and thus they probably do not offer any real security and serve rather as a means to identify possessions as mine more than to protect them: they are tokens by which my possessions lay a kind of claim in me, there are the keys to my possessing self. And thus as I stared at them on the glass in the soft light of the lamp I imagined myself approaching a lock with my keys in hand and looking down at my open palm and pausing a second in order to select the one correct key—to the car, to the back door, to the padlock—in that seemingly insignificant ritual that announces to anyone watching that whatever I am about to insert the key inside of is mine, or most probably mine.

So in an unthinking sense I had divested myself, in emptying keys from a pants pocket, or more than I had first realized, as perhaps revealed by that sense of loss first in seeing them there naked on the glass and then also by the recollection of what it felt like to walk around having momentarily lost my keys (it happened once on the beach), that sense of desolation and dispossession of being with out them spread throughout my body—the brief questioning of that peculiar right to wander through a city on foot or by car toward a fixed place, anonymous to all others, which I could identify as my car, my door, my box, my vault, by following the secret routes as pointed along by these little darts of brass and steel. And when I thought about it—the vastness of space I had taken refuge from in my darkened apartment that Friday evening—there was something almost miraculous about how in order to gain entrance to it, amid the whole city and its far-flung suburbs, I had need to find such a tiny slot into which I had to fit, right way up, a small probe of metal. The smallness of the key slot in relation to the billions or trillions of square feet of surface area in a large city—point which I can home in on with my key—while at the same time, out on the beach, I have no need to identify any one rock, any one grain of sand, any one lump of seaweed from any other, from day to day, or even hour to hour—these thoughts held me immobile inside the rectangular spaces of my apartment, while outside its wall the wind swirled, and the surf tumbled.

Then, next door, through the kitchen wall, came one of those occasional dull thuds that told me the neighbor couple were at home.

○

The smallest brass key on the ring, the one to the padlock of the storage locker, was the newest of the lot. I had just changed the lock so was aware of the brighter yellow-orange of the sheen of recent stamping and milling which had not yet given way to the dull, diffused glint of wear.

The storage locker lies a five- or six-mile drive from the apartment, out the back door and down the one-way street, more like a wide alleyway ending in the cement-paved four-lane boulevard that dead-ends at the beach to the west and whose far eastern end I have never driven to. The boulevard angles this way and that a couple of miles to the expressway, passing under it, and you can either turn left at the first signal and go north on it or drive to the next signal and turn left there and take a slower and more leisurely four-lane street lined with automotive supply stores, salvage yards, and machine shops. The storage buildings are a couple of miles to the right under a sign that reads "EZ Storage Plaza"—a warren of low cement-block structures with rows of identical corrugated steel doors set amid narrow alleyways whose pavement slopes from the walls towards a series of drainage grates set in the center of the asphalt.

On my next to the last visit a month ago I had noticed that many of the padlocks adjoining my stall were of the same brand, and I became concerned that the grooves and notches on my key might be identical to one of the others—perhaps even to several. There are two hundred and some stalls, each slightly smaller than a typical garage space. Perhaps half of these were secured with my brand of padlock. I don't know the mathematical possibilities of this matter, but even if astronomical, it still seemed to me that the normal assurances I could issue to myself might not hold, in this barren colony of identical steel doors. Two weeks later I changed the lock for a less common brand.

The storage locker door, which opens noisily upward on tracks, and the metal trim around the opening, as well as the cement blocks of the narrow strips of masonry which separate my stall from its neighbors to the right and left, and the flashing that marks the upper edge of the wall—all are painted the same slightly pinkish tan, which is flaking here and there on the metal surfaces. The glare and the heat of the place on a clear afternoon are almost unbearable. I often think of that door, locked closed, and the odor of heat-softened asphalt, feel it underfoot, and hear the ticking sound of the corrugated doors baking in the heat, as I did now standing near the chest of drawers in the bedroom. I think of the rippling bars of its horizontal corrugations glaring in the hot sun, as if there is something behind it—as if, were I to bend over and unlock the padlock and back its hasp out of the latch and grip the door handle and lift, roll it clatteringly up, there would be something behind it other than the bare cave of unpainted cement blocks, and a cement floor marked with fine cracks and puddling stains and black scuff marks, and along the far wall even rows of cardboard boxes containing those objects I periodically exile from my apartment but have been unable to throw away. I no longer remember what is in most of those boxes except old clothes.

○

I was suddenly troubled by the car key, and surprised as well, because it seemed only a few moments ago I had wandered among thoughts about the car with what had seemed like calm objectivity. True, a pang had gripped me the instant I first reached into my right pants pocket and felt the tips of my fingers butting up against the metallic points and closing around them, retrieving them with a jangling noise into the air. I had sensed that I was disturbing something that would not easily return to rest. But only keys, I had told myself. Yet I could not restrain myself from thinking of that so often repeated sequence of gestures, invariably exciting in a rising, swelling sort of way, that always leads me back through the kitchen and out the back door, down the redwood steps and straight into the alley, and then around the corner of the building into the garage, where I slip into the shadows and press the unlock button on the zapper, illuminating the interior of the car and snapping open the locks. I pull the door handle and swing open the door as far as it will go without touching the rough cement block wall, and dip my head and right foot into the space vaguely fragrant of plastic and clothing or luggage, and swivel my body in, settle into the seat, reach out and pull closed the door. Once inside I never pause in placing the key in the ignition, the other hand brushing in a confirming way to check that the shift is in park, giving the key a clockwise twist almost simultaneously. The slam-closing of the door and the urgent quick revolution of the starter motor and the reflections in the glass of the windshield, which looks out on a blank cement block wall, all immediately reassure me that I have made it once again, safe and sound, back into this refuge, and that all will be well—for the moment. But then the moment is all I ask for, just this moment of the closing of the door and the starting of the engine.

Not that the remainder, the drive and whatever else, counts for nothing at all. It does, but in the wear and fatigue and disappointment of all destination and the failure of all reaching, it may count finally less than the moment of entrance and release into this interior capsule of glass and plastic and little colored lights that go on and off, and the obedient controls of this animal-like shell or nest that I alone have the key to, this refuge from it all. I have always driven for the sake of it, not to get somewhere else: my car delivers me up to somewhere else too intact and whole of myself for there to be any destination other than this point of departure, this apartment, and I depart and arrive, go away and come back in my car in the manner of one, no more, who turns on a TV set and who watches for a time and then turns it off, finding himself sitting in a chair in an empty, silent room, just where he has always been.

It must have taken some time to sink in—that to be in this way separated from my car key, as I would be for the rest of the night and perhaps longer, was a matter of closing off the way to what I now realized was my most important, or second-most important, refuge.

○

My wallet is companion to my keys, much in the way my watch and ring are to each other, and when I take one along with me out on a walk or drive I must take the other too, so inseparable are they—though I have been known to forget my wallet and now and then will deliberately leave it on the chest of drawers when I decide to go for a long run on the beach.

I long ago purged it of all marks of spurious individuality— a playing card, a two-dollar bill connected to some adolescent event, meaningless membership cards—and now it contains only my driver's license and a single debit card.

I have always resented the business of having to carry things around in pockets. A set of keys, a handkerchief, a wallet, in certain moods, can make me feel like a beast of burden. And when I notice another male obviously pleased to display his walk and manner of dress and grooming in a public place, I will not— as almost a last point before that inevitable moment when our glances lock and then swing away from each other—how much he will have distorted himself by stuffing his pockets.

It was clear of course that I had come home that evening more laden with such impedimenta than I considered desirable in others—or at least as I inspect and compare them to some ideal as we pass each other out on the street or on the beach or wherever, though this is not the sort of judgment my eye can practice towards those framed in the windows of passing cars, where the shape of sunglasses and curve of lips and nose must stand as parts for the imagined whole, at least when not screened by tinted glass, in those strangely intimate moments in heavy slow traffic, when windows are open. And it was true that the version of myself returning home at five-thirty this evening was a somewhat bedraggled and even sloppy violation of my high standards. I offered myself the usual excuses: end of the week, a largely sleepless night out on the town about which I had been untypically anxious in advance, thus stocking my pockets like some kind of squirrel with provisions I would probably never have any use for. A handkerchief even—when I am the sort of person who rarely ever needs one.

My wallet, yes—or more exactly the removable card holder I usually slip into left shirt pocket when I want to travel lightly through the dark hours. But when the moment came that I needed to present the card and also, for some unexplained reason, my driver's license, still in my wallet, I was able to reach back and snatch the wallet out of its rear pocket with the tips of my fingers, in a casual sweep, not fumbling, not bunching up shoulders or going through the other contortions that often disfigure an otherwise promising sense of form and presence.

Perhaps even with too much elegance—because the young man at the cash register, an out-of-work or beginning actor, I would guess, perhaps a college student, who had his own dashing way of going about the confining tasks of his work, narrowed his eyes at my license and at the name or photo, and looked up, his momentarily open face a beam in search of something familiar. From the depths of the dark space an explosion of deep laughter rose up over the music. Then his eyes glazed over, dropped, narrowed to the sound the almost inaudible click of keys typing in some number, and he murmured absently while glancing to his left in the direction of the bar, "Was everything alright, sir?"

The "sir" stung. I said nothing while I signed the proffered paper slip.

○

My driver's license photo is one I have of course no control over. No one cares about the lighting of the straight-on flat-faced position of the camera—least of all the office clerks who must rush thousands of people through the procedure each year. The only way for such a photo to turn out halfway presentable would be for me to apply a heavy mask of makeup over my face—or in other words to make a fool of myself standing in line and then sitting in the bare cubicle in front of the wretched black machine, which appeared to be housed in a sort of open suitcase, a portable instrument of torture to the vain.

I am that—no doubt. Thus the special shame when I am out on the street having to carry in my wallet pressed to the hollow of my right buttock, or in my left shirt pocket, a photo whose washed out greenish tinges suggest that it was shot through a cloudy aquarium. Even the blue-black shirt I wore open at the collar could not discipline its dumb glass eye, and my features float, detached, in a sea of bleached flesh.

"I'm sorry, sir, we can't do them over again unless they don't come out," the clerk said. She was made up as a clown with freckles and huge painted lips. It was—oddly—Halloween.

I was on the edge of suggesting that indeed, exactly, precisely, it had not "come out"—but I said nothing and turned on my heels, heavily sliding under my palm the plasticized card across the counter with a hiss that made the other clerks—also bizarrely costumed—a witch, a zombie, a gorilla, Superman— twist around in their chairs and stare.

"Who was that?" they would have all been asking the moment the glass door closed on my heels.

○

Beltless, pockets emptied, jeans riding lightly on hips, I padded barefoot around the living room and into the kitchen and back again and again in the dim light, while lost in these reflections. The route took me across an expanse of oak flooring and around the perimeter of a sand-colored rug and then on a peninsular excursion in and out of the narrow kitchen with its smooth yet slightly sticky linoleum floor. How many times do you have to relive these experiences? And when do you know you can stop? I pace often when coming home, even after a long walk, to slow myself down, in the manner of a rotor coming to rest after a flight—I suppose. The light from the north window, which looks over the gray sand hillocks of a large vacant lot, was the leaden tone of dusk turning to dark. When the streetlights came on it would grow faintly lighter.

I made a joke about my driver's license photo some weeks later to my dermatologist while he was going over my skin in search of those little spots, two of which he had found a year before. "Don't tell me what they are," I had said. "I am not one of those who want to know." He had said that their removal would leave only the merest flecks as scars.

What I don't want to know is how the universe proposes to get rid of me if left to its own devices. Of course I object to the fact that it does, sooner or later. But room must be made. The preparations are long. Little spot, little bump, something sneaked into that general thickening and coarsening and weighing down of people I seem now to be acutely aware of and which has not yet—other than the two spots—begun to show itself in my body.

He said nothing. A slight intake of breath into the nostrils perhaps indicating acknowledgement of the joke, lame as I now think of it, or acknowledgement that I had spoken about something not entirely relevant to his examination, which he was too intent on, as was proper, to allow himself to be distracted from.

Gravity is what does it. You see people walking around bent over almost double, flesh sagging, everything pulled down by the force of gravity tugging away year after year. I hardly feel it. In fact despite growing suspicious I probably still feel, as opposed to believe, that it is a benign force like sunlight, which my dermatologist tells me to keep out of. But there is no way to "keep out of" gravity. Nor is there any doctor who addresses the effects of gravity upon the body, who attempts to correct the conditions I see all around me, a gravitologist. Perhaps someday there will be chambers in which you lie for several hours each day, to reverse the effects.

Then I recalled that not long before the first visit to my dermatologist I had been sunbathing in a secluded part of a mountain park where it was considered acceptable to be nude, when lying there on the grass, in an opening in the soughing pines, it began to rain lightly in the bright sun, from a cloud drifting to the east but which didn't obscure the sun on my part of the slope. I lay there spread-eagle and felt the shower of drops pricking my sweating body, sharp yet cool as they evaporated, and sensed a map of nerve-endings the patterings drew over my form. Eyelids and nose and lips were the most tingling under each splashing impact, and my lazily lolling cock, flopped to one side, not erect, but not hiding either, and my fingers—while the rest of my torso and arms and legs were barely sensitive to the drops, and my feet could almost not feel them at all. The shower passed. I sat up. I let myself dry in the sun and then dressed and hiked back down the grassy slope to my car.

That is how it will be done, I later thought. A drop at a time. A beam or a ray at a time, hurled from outer space. I will not notice them because they will seem to fall at such long intervals. Along with that endless, hardly noticed tugging from the core of the earth. Unless I do something about it first.

Such were my thoughts, as back in the bedroom, I unbuttoned my jeans and slipped them off of first my right leg and then with little kicks, with gravity assisting, from my left leg, knee raised high at the end.

I tossed them on the bed, where they lay pouchily inflated here and there by the pressures of my form, with radial creases, almost telescoping, around the knees.

○

When the dermatologist found the first spot, I imagined a beam or particle or quantum—or whatever—streaking across the universe at the speed of light, over the course of millions of light years, to home in on that point on my forehead where it was destined to collide, at some moment when I would be out walking on the beach, in the afternoon, innocently stepping through the intersection of all the coordinates. The first blow. I would not even have felt it.

It was bound to happen. The evidence is persuasive. Even though year after year I appeared to be spared well beyond the time such marks begin to show in others, those creases around eyes and mouth, lines like scars down cheeks and jowls, on the forehead between the eyes, just above the nose, that looseness and slackness in the skin in certain lights, rippled in the way that a breeze will gust down and spoil the glaze of water on a calm sea; or that veiny flush that marks the smoker's neck and arms; opening, gaping pores; blotches.

I am a student of such signs. Not that I spend more time at the mirror than another—I am not anxious to read them in myself. I once assumed they appeared in others first, perhaps even only in others. I can enter a room full of people or walk down the beach and instinctively classify those to whom it has happened and those to whom not, and then sub-divide that latter down into those who do not matter and those who do, and so on down to an individual or two of either sex who have been so far spared or have evaded the targetings of the universe, and who stand there radiantly unscathed, in the full flush of their beingness, on the very edge of the precipice, pretending to be oblivious of the fast-approaching moment when they will be ever so lightly nicked or struck or pierced by the beam or ray, or whatever, that will announce the term of their mortality.

But I have always really known, even when I wondered why I seemed so long spared. I knew all the signs as well as my dermatologist, lacking only the floodlights and magnifying lenses. It was I who found the thing, a persistent roughness on my forehead that refused to be rubbed or washed away. Where I had been banged or nudged or poked by the needle of time. I could not ask him why. How, yes, and he would have plenty of droning explanation, the middle-aged doctor, with the spotless while lab coat masking his paunch, the pressed and starched material warm to the touch—as in his investigations he butted against my bare arm, while I lay shirtless on the table; but never why. I knew the answer, as I said. To make room. But such a waste, I thought. All this trouble gone to, and then it's over.

Or not quite over. I would live out my life having to pretend. That I had not been marked or stricken. I would have five years of not being seriously questioned. In ten, I knew, I would inspire in those who knew me a kind of admiration for how I managed to maintain appearances. In twenty, with hard work, I would be regarded as a kind of precious, fragile object, rare and startling, for which elaborate arrangements are made in advance of its movements. And after that—but why bother to think?

O

I stood in the living room in front of the round bezel of the thermostat. In the dim light I thought I could make out the little triangle that serves as a pointer nudging seventy degrees. The air was cool on my bare legs. I could feel the hairs spring free, released from their former confinement. I twisted the dial counterclockwise to seventy-five. The electric baseboard heat is slow to change but even in its heating. In an instant the elements or fins began ticking, a crisp pricking sound against the dull roar of the distant surf.

A blue-gray light filled the room. I had lost track of the time but would not seek it out. I was here after all to wallow in a last abundance of it, not measure it out. If I happened back into the bedroom, as surely I would, and if I happened to glance at my watch on the chest of drawers, supposing I had left it face up, then I would perhaps notice the time—but I wouldn't go in for the purpose of checking on it. The grayness of the light from both the south and north windows of the living room, both uncurtained, suggested it was somewhat before eight—for whatever that was worth. The last joggers and walkers would have left the beach for the sea walk, or even the residential streets and alleys of this stretch of the coast, and the gulls and sandpipers and other shore birds would have sought out their roosts or protected perches. I had no wish to be outside yet in the embrace of the clammy air. The ticking heaters made me feel momentarily content in their presence, indoors, inside, even as my mind persisted in wandering up and down the deserted beach.

It was, I realized, the last wear I would have of those jeans, no matter what. I padded back into the bedroom and approached the bed and looked down on them: yes, they were the pair. Or the last wear to work or out on any occasion when I wished to appear at the top of my form. I had noticed a small stain near the knee, blackish, something not likely to wash out, a speck of grease perhaps picked up while getting in or out of the car, or one of those nameless lumps of gelatinous matter flicked up in the course of walking across a parking lot. The denim was also beginning to show the first signs of thinness and limpness and fatigue beyond what I consider acceptable. They would be relegated now to beach walks on cold days or house-cleaning or car-cleaning chores or shopping at the supermarket. Three other pair lay folded in the bottom drawer of the chest of drawers, only one of which I had tried on for size in the in the flimsy paneled changing room of the clothing store I shop at—if only to confirm that my waist size had not changed. But I had been in no hurry on that lazy afternoon in late autumn, and the clerk was friendly but not overly solicitous, and he urged me to have free run of the empty store—while he went about some business involving a touchpad, something to do with inventory or orders, over which he hunched, flicking his red tie out of the way, and exposing a small bald patch in the tight whorls of his short blond hair. The severe admonitions on the changing booth door, Shoplifting is a Crime, Only Three Garments at a Time, were not for me, I knew, and for once I tried on the jeans without feeling I was about to be burst in on by a red-faced mother and her fat adolescent boy, or disturbed by someone impatiently wrenching at the locked knob. The jeans fit, of course. The clerk was in some other world, when I handed him the debit card, and was whistling to himself, gaze, periodically rising to the far-off destination he was piloting this vast empty enclosure toward, and all these wardrobes, and for an instant or two, I supposed, whoever else of us happened to be aboard.

O

I had loosened my tie but not taken it off. The knot dangled a few inches below the unbuttoned collar which flared out away from my neck while at the same time was pulled back in place by the tabs, still buttoned down, and though I did not at first remember it, I must also have unbuttoned the top button of my shirt in order to enable the reaming motion by which at last I was able to free my neck from the embrace of those eight hours plus at work. A curve of T-shirt would show in the mirror, a dark blue, almost black crescent just below the twin points of collarbone.

And now, in untying the knot and tugging the tie counter-clockwise from my neck with the hissing of the rough material of the tie against the smoother weave of the inside of the collar, I recalled the quick moment of tying the knot and cinching ever so slowly the loop tighter and tighter around my neck, closing the gap in the collar to the point where its two ends overlapped just enough to give the impression that the collar button was fastened. It was a day I could not live through with a buttoned collar, I clearly remember deciding in advance. Then I would be easily able to loosen the tie some eight or nine hours later, I could reason, car started and moving through the parking lot, wheels dropping over the edge of the cement ramp into the gutter of the boulevard, head craning left to wait for the traffic to open: moment when I would have noticed the constraint around my neck and would have realized that now, at last, after these eight hours, I could begin to release it. Yet I often delayed. Had I this afternoon?

I have been told that I have a relatively long neck for my height, with finely bearded skin, lightly pebbled as with goose bumps, which stretches over well-defined cords and veins and a prominent Adam's apple, and which projects, or so I have reason to believe, a strong, almost riveting presence—at least perhaps on those too rare occasions when I throw back my head and bare my neck to view. I cannot think of putting anything so tightly around my neck for any reason except to festoon it—though always in a restrained way that would not distract from the upright, forever firm column of flesh and bone and pulsating artery which lies exposed to view.

A tie in that sense is perfect, and this particular one was of a course knit, a dark navy blue so close to black that in most lights you could not be certain; and with squared ends, it was one of those ties that goes in and out of fashion, in and out of being retro. It tied into a swelling square knot, like a fist, almost too large for my collar size, which is relatively small. There was something slightly daring in the largeness of the knot, which perhaps called added attention to the arched expanse of neck. When wearing it I have often noticed a slight hesitation after people begin addressing me with the usual rote-like questions, as if adjusting their expectations to a new reality; though later, afterward, I imagine that the perception was so miniscule as to be quickly forgotten or else merged into a sense of heightened alertness that some encounters cause to flare into being—and which would translate at most into lingering a few seconds longer than expected, perhaps into a trivial question concerning the lateness of the hour or the weather or the outcome of a national sporting event.

I store my ties on a rack in the shadowy depths of the right side of the closet. After inspecting this one for signs that it might need cleaning and finding none, I walked, toes curled up against the cold of the waxed boards, or rather hobbled, over to the open doors and reached inside with my left hand and draped the length of rough material over a plastic-tipped steel rod near the top of the rack. My hand brushed against some of the other dozens of ties I own, in one of those instants of absolute silence in the apartment, when surf and wind had paused, and I could hear the different registers of material, some smooth and silken, others coarsely knit with miniscule strands of fine grasping tendrils, brushing against the back of my wrist. Then the walls reverberated and the floor creaked.

○

By all rights of course I should have slipped off the tie the moment I stepped out the door from work, but most often I would only loosen it a little, deep into the parking lot or climbing into the hot, fragrant interior of the car, and sometimes I would wait until I was out on the boulevard, almost halfway home, and rarely I would wait even later than that.

Putting it on in the morning was always an agony, in the recurring fear that I would forget how to make the knot—which occasionally I have done, whereupon I have had to calm myself, sit down, nibble at a cracker, or even lie down briefly, and think of something else. I cannot stand to have anything tight around my neck, which means that I have to go through each working day in a state of low-level distress held in check only by means of loquacious lectures to myself how it is all in the mind, urgings to think of something else, and so on, and by seeking the refuge of banter with my co-workers—who behave also with this false cheer because perhaps they are equally disturbed by this noose around the neck or by some other constraint imposed by the sclerotic management.

But the difficulty of putting it on—the knot—in the morning was matched by an odd reluctance at times to slip it off at the end of the day, perhaps because of the slow, patient labor of having got used to it one more time—and almost a reluctance to experience again the thrill of an open, free collar. Thus, perversely, I sometimes kept it on until the last possible moment, until I would experience the ridiculous vision of myself in a mirror, in the apartment, tie still on tight, mark of my submission to all that which I so deeply seek to evade.

○

The wind buffeting the building dropped for a moment, per-haps while it wheeled around to another direction, and in that moment there came a lull in the distant surf, and for the first time since I had come home that evening, I heard the throbbing roar of traffic on the highway to the east, or half heard, half felt through the thin stucco walls. I remained inside the shadowy closet. Then the wind resumed, and the building creaked, and in that instant I remembered I had left something in the rear right pocket of my jeans, which lay rumpled on the bed. It came back to me in a flash: a solitary envelope, a bill, or statement rather of the monthly electricity charge being automatically debited from my bank account. Yet I could remember no more. Frozen in place I strained to remember the gesture by which I would have flipped open the lid of the mailbox with the back of my left wrist and groped around in the smooth metal pocket with extended fingers until their tops would have brushed up against the rigid paper form of the rectangular envelope before closing on it. Surely this would have been at about six, on my way up-stairs from the garage, which is when I usually collect the scant mail. I would have noticed that there was no other mail, which would have been usual—because though I could not recall paus-ing on the steps and swiveling around to face the mailbox, I still remained certain from some source that there had been no other mail except the electricity statement, which I had chosen not to open, and none of the advertisements and solicitations which I occasionally also receive.

I freed myself from this puzzle and padded over to my jeans. Perhaps I was confusing this evening with another time. But no, the envelope was there. It had been bent into a slightly domed shape by having remained in the pocket pressed against my right buttock. I withdrew it an studied the faint contour. The corners of the envelope had also been blunted in the brief though humid confinement, and an oblique wrinkle spanned the face, cutting irregularly across my name and address. I carried it through the living room and into the kitchen and placed it at the end of the laminated counter. The contour still held. Why could I not recall removing it from the box? As it lay there, corners bent up, the thought came to me that it was like a piece of skin that had slaked off, or a plate or a scale, like some insentient part of my body.

○

A growing fullness in my bladder finally focused itself into a more pointed urging, and I returned to the bathroom, slipped down the elastic front of my briefs and flipped out my penis—I am no more comfortable with that somewhat formal name for it than any of a half dozen others, and think of it simply most often as "it"—and urinated. I often imagine the yellow plume proceeding down the plumbing and into the sewer and through the treatment plant, which is up the coast and inland a ways, and then out into the ocean, gradually dispersing and fading into the clear waters. It would not happen quite that way, of course: the reality must be far more churning and confused. And yet as I stand, bladder draining its last drops, in the immobile and contemplative stance facing the blank part of the wall next to the wash basin, it is the picture that most often comes to mind.

Finished, I pulled the elastic band back up, and pressed the chrome-plated lever that swirled and then sped these several ounces of my fluids towards the ocean. A gargling sound from the toilet bowl, as I stepped back into the bedroom, told me the flush had completed; there would follow then the long contented sigh of the plumbing as the tank slowly refilled itself.

○

Some gulls were flying low overhead, their deep throated caws followed by hinge-like wheezings. They would have been driven back from the beach by the wind, perhaps too high for them to scout for garbage, and the pier to the south would have been empty of fishermen most of the afternoon. It bothered me to have forgotten in my excitement the details of picking up the mail not because the act had some obscure importance but because I took pleasure in the little gestures and habits of my life, and thus to forget one before its time, as it were, was a serious omission. I could easily say to myself that it didn't matter but then I might soon be accidentally losing track of whole sequences of daily habit, and perhaps even days at a time. I have the impression that I could remember every day I have lived, and though I cannot say exactly where this memory resides I know that given enough time I could relive much of my life minute by minute. But why would I want to do something like that, when so much of the effort of my life lies in forgetting? Still, I was troubled by the loss of these ten seconds or so, and it seemed no small matter, because perhaps they had slipped away without my willing them to disappear.

O

While unbuttoning my shirt, I set about pacing the U-shaped length of the apartment, which I often do in order to help me puzzle through a problem or recall something that has slipped my mind, adding something like an extra step by brushing my foot against the floor between proper steps, particularly when my feet are bare. Indoors, this serves to slightly slow my course, thus prolonging the time it takes for each lap and thus softening the absurdity of taking what often seems like a long walk in a confined space, but it also recalls how I often walk through shallow surf, in the white foam, at the end of a warm, clear day, how with toes splayed wide I plow through the hissing and bubbling water. The evening was humid and the dampness of having been confined to shoes and socks still seemed to cling to my soles, so that my pacings were accompanied by little squeaks and grunts and groans of friction between flesh and newly waxed floor, and, as I heeled around at the corner where the bookcase stood in the living room, and the low coffee table and lamp, there came a singing gasp. At the other end of my loop the hardwood gave way to quieter linoleum with an incised or embossed pattern imitating ceramic tiles of some traditional design.

I slowly unbuttoned my shirt, left cuff first, then right, allowing sleeves to float free up to nearly the elbows, and then the top button below the collar, by inserting thumbnail under the finely woven blue material and running it up into the buttonhole and then with index finger pushing the button through. This I did with the right hand one at a time, down the six or seven buttons as I paced. Like the jeans, the shirt was a older one I had bought a year or so before men's store whose shirt display was presided over by a slight, bony old man who walked with stomach thrust forward, in the manner of someone much larger and heavier, and who spoke with the scratchy voice of the aged. He briskly sold me three shirts when I had intended to buy only one.

I never went back, though by now perhaps he has retired and been replaced by someone younger. There was something embryonic about his reddish, almost transparent skin, his baldness even, and his presence haunted me, almost inhabited me for days until I was able to shake myself free of it. I tend to swallow people I meet casually, some people at least, not all. It is as if they enter into my being and take over the way I walk and move and even the way I hear myself talk, and for several days after having only the briefest dealings with the old man he worked determinedly within me as if I was his puppet—and I seemed to walk like him, with his waddling stomach-thrust-out manner, and I could hear the scratchy voice in my own throat, and when I looked in the mirror I could barely see anything of myself, only that veiny transparent skin, the baldness. There is nothing I can do to expel these impersonations, which last usually about three days, and from which I can suddenly awake at any moment, the burden sloughing off as suddenly as it was first assumed.

But all of this comes back, if only fleetingly, whenever I put on or take off the shirt or either of its two companions. I have often been tempted to throw them away. Yet I bought them of my own free will, whatever the skill of the old man in selling them to me, and they fit exceptionally well, snug without being tight, and nowhere do they bind. Yet I wear them only when I have exhausted all the other shirts I regularly wear, partly out of the recollection of the old man who sold them to me, even though I have passed well beyond the time when I felt his presence under my skin directing my gestures and movements—none of which

I'm sure would have been noticeable to anyone around me, any-one at the office, in anything more than an unusual hesitation in gesture or in a sentence uncharacteristically trailing off unfin-ished. At worst, I would have been perceived as being slightly under the weather or otherwise distracted.

The memory of those days is still there, however, like the faintest of odors. The shirt and its companions are the ones I will often not wash, the ones I will leave rumpled in the bottom of the closet, particularly when my laundry bag is too full and when I do not want to load a second machine; yet even in this there is a kind of snag, as the pleasure I take in washing my clothes, shirts especially, even while preceded by a wave of reluctance and even aversion, lies largely in that sense of washing out these impersonations which against my will I must assume. Something in the turbulance of the machine, the sloshing around of soapy water, mixes them all up and carries them away, out to sea, and for a time at least I can walk with a lighter step. To leave in the bottom of the closet this shirt and its two companions is thus to delay the very washing which will cleanse them of their origins, at least temporarily.

I thought then that when the moment came I would quite deliberately peel off the shirt and stuff it into my half-full laun-dry bag so that I would be sure to take it to the laundromat the next trip in a week or so, knowing that I would later go to the trouble of fishing it out to make room for some more valued or less tainted laundry—while marveling at my deep persistence in making useless little plans.

○

But not yet. I was taking pleasure in the unbuttoned shirt flowing after me like a cape, bare feet skipping across the oak floor, carpet, floor, linoleum and back. The first faint but sharp odor of perspiration mixed with the sweetish smell of deodorant had dissipated, and once again I was aware of passing in and out of zones of various domestic odors, that of bread perhaps in the kitchen area, or the smell of baking that persisted still into my time from the previous tenants, underlying a sharper almost vinegary scent from something decaying in the plastic garbage bin under the sink, and then an almost neutral, somewhat dusty emanation from the living room area, and around the corner another sharp sensation of clothing or bedding or perhaps the residues of cleaning fluids and detergents. My course took me to the foot of the rumpled unmade bed, where the jeans lay spread out, and almost to the open closet, but not as far as the bathroom door, out of which I knew would billow the sweetish smell of the bathroom cleaner I had used two days before—were I to approach closely enough to ruffle the still air.

I paced for five minutes or so though at one point I became so lost in the rhythms of the walk and the trick by which I ended up with the right amount of paces at each end of the trajectory that I would not have to make a half-step or take one too long, so as to step at just the right—if arbitrary—place before wheeling around, at the foot of the bed and at the kitchen table—that I lost track of time. Gradually it came back to me that the day before I had stopped for gas on the way home from work, which had made me late, and that in my rush up the stairs and back down again I had forgotten the mail. which turned out to be nothing more than the electricity statement which I had fished out of the box early this morning and had stuffed into my right rear pocket, where it had traveled through the day. I would have been half asleep. My encounter with the mail box would have been hurried, thoughtless, and I would have uncharacteristically not even paused to open the envelope, in order perhaps pointlessly to save those few seconds which somehow might add up into the minutes which I knew would be necessary to arrive at work exactly when I prefer to. In then a kind of mental simulacrum of haste, I would have tossed away the memory of these small events.

Yesterday evening, the gas pump having refused to give me a receipt and thus forcing me to go inside, I had hit upon the moment when the shifts were being changed, and a dark older woman with bright almost lavender lipstick was exchanging cash trays with a younger, chubby woman with a round face and who seemed confused by all she suddenly had to keep track of. At my back through the open glass doors came the hiss of a steady stream of traffic on the warm pavement and the sounds of car doors opening and closing and of gas pumps being started and shut off, under the high steel canopy. I felt the seconds leak away as the fat young woman puzzled out the numbers she was to punch into the cash register. The woman in line in front of me held a sack of potato chips that crackled with her slightest movement. She cradled it in her arms like a baby, the better to hold out a twenty-dollar bill. I could feel the faint stretching of skin to the pulsations in my neck. The drive to and from the office is purposefully long: half the city lies between the inland suburb where I work and my apartment on the beach, which is the way I would have it, that distance, which gives my punctualities an almost heroic edge—overcoming these small barriers. Despite this one, and others, I arrived home within minutes of my usual time.

O

So forgetting to pick up the mail on my way up the stairs in the evening on the way home from work had already become a habit: this evening I had done exactly the same thing, and the mail, if there was any, even if worthless, lay in the shallow black metal box at the bottom of the railing, and I was faced with the question of whether I should scamper barefoot and bare-legged down the staircase in the cold wind to retrieve the perhaps damp envelopes, risking the quizzical glance of an unlikely passerby. If there was nothing I would feel foolish and weak at having submitted to my curiosity for some trivial reward. There would be no letters, only statements, junk mail with tired, unbelievable images of other places or things I had no need for—and yet as I would flip back the lid, which grated sharply, I would always be led to complete the gesture by the faintest thread of hope that somehow the randomness of things might deliver into that box some word, some image that might change everything. Did I still hold that possibility?

No, it was a trap—set up no doubt by my too clever forgetfulness, to lure me away from this moment by surprising me out of my determination in the suddenly bracing air, or to confuse me with annoyance or anger that once having got up my hopes to tramp down the wooden stairs in darkness I would reach into the box and find it quite empty.

Yet I would now wonder, I knew, throughout the evening and into the early hours of the morning about what might be or not be in the mailbox, and there would be a busy little part of me that would plot how to step outside and walk down those stairs and back up without the rest of me paying much attention. Would it finally be fatigue or resignation or absent-mindedness that would grant permission to step outside?

O

I completed these thoughts while pausing to stare absently at the bed, which I had as usual failed to make that morning. Its top sheet lay flung back over the white bedspread, all I ever slept under, and the jeans lay sprawled across the white expanse oddly like a sunbathing figure on a beach, or perhaps in a form that recalled how I at one time had tossed them on the sand of a remote beach I sometimes drive and hike to in order to spend a solitary day in the sun. It stretches for miles but because of its remoteness and a peculiarity in the low choppy waves of the surf the beach is not much used except by solitary sunbathers like myself, who position themselves at distant but oddly regular intervals. I spend the day, as I assume others do, by dozing and turning in the sun, and now and then squinting into the heat haze at my companions, who are close enough that I can make out that they are mainly men though with a sprinkling of women, as naked as I am, but too far to decipher an expression or glance, other than the rituals of turning, stretching, putting on and taking off sunglasses, rubbing on sunscreen or some other lotion, and periodic strolls to the water for quick dips. One does not linger in the cold water because the bottom drops off sharply into rocks; rusty signs warn of dangerous currents. A day passes thus. My body stretches out and expands to fill the whole bright landscape and finally, throbbing and weary in the sun and wind, becomes faint and dizzy with the uncertainty of where the edge is of what I am in this glistening body on the bright sand. Late afternoons I must slip clothes, which feel rough and scratchy, back on and begin hiking back to the car before dark. I think of the others by then as a herd of sea-going animals, my kind, even though we are rarely close enough to recognize an expression, or hear a sound of each other—a distance I carefully maintain, even as I squint throughout the day across the sand.

○

The bed was unmade, as it always was up until that moment in the late evening or early morning I habitually went to bed and pulled the top sheet and gray quilted bedspread into place, straightening them carefully at the top of the bed, sheet pulled back over the edge of the bedspread so as to make a neat, even line. I cannot sleep with anything touching my neck and chin except that precise edge—no wadded rumple of sheet and blanket pushing up like a muffler—or rather barely touching, lying a fraction of an inch away from my skin, and making only enough contact here and there, now and then to assure me that the edge has held through the night, though by morning I can be occasionally oblivious to the state of the bedding, and even not mind finding it pulled halfway up over my face, in reaction to some dream or nightmare.

I buy new sheets every six months as a matter of course, for the feel of them: an old sheet gone limp and clinging, its whiteness beginning to dim, can give me a sleepless night—as perhaps a too vivid reminder of the inexorable processes of wear. I feel younger in fresh sheets, more alert, and can relax more readily at the end of the day—in fact, I have been more than once about to explain to the various sales clerks at the stores where I have bought them, only at the last minute fortunately thinking better of it. The clerk at the last place seemed to remember that I had bought quite a lot of sheets there, at least to judge from her queries. She was short and dark and had a way of looking at me almost placidly with her wide-set eyes while chatting away. "You prefer this brand, do you? We sell a lot of these even though they are more expensive, but they do last." Her skin was almost waxy. "You don't see men buying sheets too often," she carried on, tapping the sale into the machine. "Women of course will buy anything. Would you sign here, please."

○

My arches had begun to ache under the effect of standing barefoot on the hard surface, and I resumed pacing, now and then raising myself to tip toes as I walked, in an attempt to restore a more normal feeling to my instep. By now the reddish marks from the elastic ribbing of my socks had faded from my feet and ankles, and the hairs had sprung free. Even though some time had passed since I had taken off shoes and socks and had slipped out of my jeans it was only now that I knew that sense of bodily freedom that comes from being without clothing after a long spell of being fully dressed. The air tingled against my bare legs. At the base of my scrotum, a tickling worm of sensation shifted, then lay quiescent again.

I paused before the open closet door, turned around, and twisted outward my left calf, to inspect a point of itchiness which was suddenly sharp enough to suggest a small biting insect, but a quick brush with my had dispelled it as one of those random bodily sensations which have no cause other than, I suppose, the restlessness of flesh. My wiry leg hairs had been worn shorter by the friction of pants legs higher up on the calf—but I could never figure out why they stopped short at the ankles, leaving the feet bare except for a trail down the ridge of the foot and sprinklings on the toes. Such patterns always suggested to me that my body had once been used in ways and for purposes I could never understand or remember—that like a tool it had once been owned by someone else, whose actions and habits had worn it in this way rather than that.

I threw back my shoulders and let the shirt slip off first one arm and then the other. Winding it up into a ball around my left wrist I stuffed into the depths of the laundry bag. It would get washed among the other clothes after all. Beyond and below the sagging muslin bag, in a dark corner of the closet there gleamed an object I couldn't recognize yet could somehow imagine nestled in the detritus of dust balls. But I turned away with investigating further, guessing only that though it was in the logical place of an unused metal shoe tree that had been left by the previous tenant, it was probably not that. Taking off a shirt has always been an admission of fatigue. As I turned and looked back across the bed to the doorway into the living room, a certain weariness came over me. I wondered what the weather was like now outside.

○

My fingers sought out the spot of itchiness once again and lingered there, at the back of the left thigh just above the knee, and found what they had skipped over before: a tiny point of roughness. I twisted around and bent back but could see nothing in the dim light of that part of the room, so I walked over to the floor lamp in the living room and lifted my leg up on to the arm of the wicker sofa and repeated the twisting motion, pushing the flesh this way and that around the spot.

"Keratosis" was the term my dermatologist had used. Was this the third one? I smoothed the skin and dropped my foot back to the floor and resumed pacing, stopping every now and then to touch the spot: yes, it was there, firmly attached or engrained or rooted. This was a blow I did not expect quite so soon. The third one, the third wound of time. He had said they were much more common in people with fair skin, but unusual in people with my kind of skin. Was it safe to leave it? Would it just keep growing, getting larger and larger, rooting deeper and deeper? Ridiculous questions of course, given how I planned to end this night—though oddly the spot seemed to be posing an odd objection, as if it had the right to grow and swell at my expense as long as it needed to, and that I had to keep myself alive and healthy to serve its purposes.

Or was it the straw I secretly hoped to find, to clutch to, like the cold or flu that intervenes with all its miseries between me and the large questions that follow me around, day and night, almost everywhere, those strange moments of relief and even happiness that come with illness? I wondered whether they executed prisoners who come down with colds the day before, or does the ceremony require perfect health? Would an emerging keratosis qualify?

I paused and turned to look at it one more time under the light. No, I thought, it is almost invisible. You are seeking straws, I said to myself. You are secretly hoping there will be a knock at the door—however unlikely this might be. You cannot become the spot. It is no refuge. Forget it.

○

I had slipped my left hand under my T-shirt and was running it slowly up and down chest and stomach to put off the moment, I suppose, of padding over to the bathroom door and switching on the light and stepping inside to stare myself down in the mirror of the medicine cabinet, and had even begun to swivel on the balls of my heels to face in that direction when a slight pressure of discomfort in my stomach, and a hardness to my palping hand just below the left rib cage, called me back to the fact of having paused briefly on my way home from work to eat something, to prepare myself for the long evening. I keep very little food in the kitchen, not being one of those creatures ruled by hunger, though I have never bothered to unplug the usually empty refrigerator, which cycles contentedly on and off through the day and night as if performing useful work. I suppose it heats the kitchen slightly.

The place was a deli-cafe in a neighborhood I drive through on the way back from work but have otherwise no connection with. I had eaten there perhaps only once or twice before, and this time was no different from those others. I arrived just after the L-shaped space had been probably jammed with a late-afternoon crowd, which had abruptly departed leaving tables littered with small white plates and stainless steel cutlery and crumpled paper napkins and wrappers; and the college- or high-school-age staff dressed in white and black, to match perhaps the checkerboard tiles of the floor, were chattily cleaning up the tables—at least until I swung in the door and stood for a time reading the blackboard menu above the deli counter, and their bright voices fell away to be replaced by the grunts of chairs and tables being dragged short distances across the polished floor, and the thumping clatter of plates and silverware being tipped into plastic bus trays. I was the only customer. I felt a lightening up my spine and around the back of the neck. Again, I thought: the heavy, vast effort of holding self together.

Nonetheless I persevered as if nothing was the matter, head cocked back, staring at the menu board above the counter as if lost in thought and unable or unwilling to decide or in no hurry to do so, the perfect bemused customer who has all the time in the world. The special sandwich would do, I thought, even though I might also have eaten it or something just like it at noon, and also the day before, and the day before that, my rule being that if choice A is on the menu I order that, and if not, then on to my choice B, and so on; and I had had the odd luck this past week to hit on a long succession of restaurants and snack bars and carts that all offered my choice A—with of course the usual variations; which is why I sought out this not quite out of the way place, in the hope that it would throw my system of choices temporarily off track.

Eventually the blonde waitress in black skirt, white blouse came around the counter and looked across at me with the generous full-lipped smile, the even teeth, she had flashed at my entrance moments earlier, and again at a table she had been reflectively cleaning up while nudging the shoulders of a tall, ramrod straight young man with unshaven red cheeks and long black eyelashes and almost wetly smoothed down straight black hair; but the focus of her eyes was a fraction on an inch off and I knew that it was deeply elsewhere, staring far away into the depths of the immortality of the present tingling moment. As I ate my choice B at a corner table somewhat darker than the others, seeming to stare into space, into the afternoon glare of the plate glass windows, I watched the two flit about the room cleaning up tables like a pair of mating birds, the big dark gangly one momentarily released from his shyness, and the smaller blond one accepting the proof of what her smile said she knew, that she would live forever young and beautiful, forever defying the force of gravity. I was their brooding witness who, along with the wire-leg tables, the glowing counters, the absent owners, levitated them into the tension of their flighty game; without us, they might have sat quiet and sullen, ruminating over the more ordinary future that the larger world, in its begrudging collectivity, held out to them. I ate quickly, left with a nod into thin air in the direction of where I thought somebody might be, and thought I would immediately forget it all forever.

My haste to return to the apartment after work had swallowed these moments of unease—or rather that steady even longing to be back in the presence of the ocean again, enclosed in rooms not far from it, even though my view is only a narrow strip of water between two stucco apartment buildings, a thin band above a lip of gray sand which is pocked with old foot marks and blotched with the scraggly forms of ice plant grasping for a toehold. It is another presence than just that pinched view that pulls me back through my days away, an almost tidal force, something emanating from the distant wallowing and washing sounds of the surf or the sharp shock of a wave that has come in close, the breeze itself pushing itself through cracks in the windows and under the door; or in the smell of the spray or fog, of the almost always gauzy light when the fog lifts. Or not so much these things as their residues I carry in memory when away. It is a huge animal I orient myself in the direction of to listen to its tossings and turnings, in no expectation other than that it will always be there; and in fact I am better perhaps at imagining it—it is a richer, more subtle creature than the one I will visit often late in the afternoon or early in the morning, when it will appear to my eye to be flat and listless or simply mechanical in its churnings, and there will be something almost weary in the patrolling gulls and sandpipers, and the light will rest dully on the foaming water. I see it better inside my apartment staring unfocused at the strip of blue or gray water between the two stucco buildings, or even staring at the blank wall to the left of the window, except perhaps at night when the ocean's rumblings and occasional glitters are as unpredictable and mysterious as my dreams—and when I sense at night that perhaps I do not know it at all, this creature, and that it is far from whatever I could imagine it to be.

And when away, deep into the city's most distant suburbs, I cannot say what it is that I miss in this presence or what it is I am longing for—have I not heard all the variations of the crash of waves or seen the light play in all its combinations?—except the gestures and murmurings of something or someone I cannot be without and have come to know as essential companion, whose presence goes back to the beginning of time—and which has become, over time, that which I always turn toward—and which I cannot long consciously think about without a tingling warmth filling arms and legs, as if I have just emerged from swimming, and the unfurling stretchings of the first signs of an erection—at the memory of the coursing waters.

I hide myself in the world, behind walls, behind steel and glass, within clothes, within even the darting movements of walking or running or driving, from those others also hiding, laboring constantly to forget. All is evasion. Yet in the ocean I no longer need hide: I am embraced, fondled, played with. I am taken for what I am, not what I seem, by the infinity of its water—to whom I give myself without fear. The ocean is my lover, which is why I must hasten home each night, to be nearby, in its presence, within hearing of its call, within sight of the glintings of its waves.

Why, it asks, do you burden yourself with body, with the human evasions, with the world?

○

I shivered at these thoughts, which until now had inhabited the inchoate edges of my mind: they had never come to me in such a direct manner. I held myself immobile, almost rigid, listening for some sound through the walls, but could sense without quite hearing only the dull roar of distant traffic. The ocean would be ruminating quietly.

But then I resumed. With arms crossed and fingers slipped under the lower hem I pulled the T-shirt up over my chest and out of shoulders and over neck and head and arms, tousling my hair in the process, in one hissing expansive movement. Then I wadded the cotton material up and carried it over to the bed where I would drop it—not in the closet—in the hope of being able to wear it one more time before tossing it in the laundry. A hesitation revealed itself at that moment, as I stood beside the bed, wadded up form held between hands, as I became aware of the warmth of my body still trapped in the folds of the soft material, and suddenly it seemed to become quite another object—like the pelt of some animal or entrails freshly removed from a carcass. I let the rumpled blue form fall from my hands. It perched on the edge for an instant, then slid off into a heap on the floor.

No, it would go into the laundry. The day had turned out warmer than I had expected, and was more humid, and I had perspired more than usual, my body complaining of being slightly overdressed much of the day, even within the air-conditioned space of the office. I had a half-dozen such T-shirts of a somewhat rare brand that did not climb the neck or bind under the arms, all dark blue, all purchased at a store where I bought nothing else—or at least until they discontinued the brand. Such shopping rituals helped me overcome the squeamishness of approaching racks of underwear and to move quickly through that passage where public goods—T-shirts, briefs, even socks—become incorporated into the intimacy of my being—an anxiety which ends precisely at that moment when the checkout clerk drops the object into a bag, and it disappears within a pastel plastic mask, and my hands fold over the top of the bag—with perhaps a last re-opening to drop in the sales slip. My last—ever, I suppose—purchase of this brand of T-shirt involved a moment of bravado when I asked why they were on sale, and the clerk, looking away, said because they were being discontinued. I murmured almost in spite of myself, "I'll take three more." And we had to go through the whole painful business again, after I quickly made my way back to the underwear counter and picked up three more blue T-shirts and handed them to the checkout clerk, a powdered older woman festooned with gold jewelry who revised the transaction on the noisy, grinding cash register—while the T-shirts were tactlessly splayed across the counter during the long and complicated business, until finally they attained the privacy of the mauve shopping bag, and the top was rolled over once again. I left wordlessly, flushed, perspiring.

○

I bent over and picked the T-shirt up off the carpet, having remembered that I had been irritated just below the left shoulder blade on and off throughout the day by probably a hair caught in the weave of the material. I turned the shirt inside out and carried it into the living room floor lamp and carefully ran my hand over the suspect area. I'd had my hair cut early in the week, Tuesday, I think, easily two changes of underwear ago, but a hair could have been transported to this particular spot through successive changes of clothes—improbably but possible. I spread out the material and held it taut against the light, tilting it this way and that, until a telltale gleam revealed itself. I drew my eye close and carefully pinched out the hair between thumbnail and nail of my index finger: it was no more than a quarter inch long, black and stiff, clearly one of my own. Its very shortness explained why I sometimes felt it, sometimes not, throughout the day. I flicked it from my fingers to the floor.

I am the perfect customer. They try to hold me, my easy-to-cut-hair, my easily shaped head, while I chafe against the forced intimacy of strange hands and arms the carefully neutral odors of the clothing of the usually young men and women who have danced slowly around my seated form, carrying on some monologue that needs feeding with no more than grunts and polite affirmations. I go to a different hair place every time, in wider and wider circles from the office. From this last time, Tuesday, for an instant I felt again the warm breath down the back of my neck of the last one, a chubby girl with a heavy jaw and wisps of dark hair like sideburns and a locket hanging from her neck from a fine gold chain, spread out across a wide shelf of breast resting upon a larger stomach. She moved her hips in a heavy pendulous sweep, almost as if dancing, and when she stepped back to survey her handiwork she would lift the gold chain between thumb and forefinger and drop it back upon the thin black sweater, as if to straighten it.

Later at the cash register—and I barely concealed my haste in bounding up out of the flimsy swiveling chair—she fastened her gaze on me just below the level of my eyes and drew back her thin lips in a tentative smile, then flicked her glance up to my eyes an instant before dropping it back to the cash register and the receipt that was emerging by short little jerks. My pen was ready, which confused her. I signed and separated her white sheet from my faintly yellowish copy and turned away. Amid the humming of the cash register and the bland music and the grind of distant hair dryers, the sound of the two copies of the receipts separating from each other was of a strange delicateness. It signaled my release from the agony once again.

○

I stood. A warm glow suffused my limbs sufficient just to balance the slight chill of the room. I found myself standing in the warmest part of the bedroom, on the carpet near the foot of the bed, a draftless spot warmed by the water heater or furnace downstairs next to the garage—enclosed in that central vault-like column that supports part of the building. One foot rested on the other, a thumb slipped into the elastic band of my briefs, the other gently scratching mid-spine behind my back, a position with variations I could assume for hours while my eyes glided over the details of the room or noted the changes in the light out the west window, a portion of which I could see from where I stood, or deciphered the crepitations of this space and made out the muffled flingings of the surf as their vibrations passed through the row of apartment buildings that masked the ocean from mine; the comings and goings of my neighbors' cars, which I knew better than my neighbors themselves—fleeting parcel- and bag-carrying apparitions, pushers of garbage carts, who like me were always scurrying off to lose themselves in the long streets and expressways or vanish into the endless expanse of white sand—or who, for all I know, also barricaded themselves within their stucco enclosures for hours on end, alone, staring into space. Now and then one of them would hold a party, and the vibrations of the music would pulsate through the windows into the early hours of the morning, while I would stand within my space and sit and pace the night through—or until I would drop from exhaustion, thus ending my vigil to see whether I would go through with whatever it was that I dared myself to do—holding on to the instant of indecision that might last for hours—listening to the arguments within myself—that I had projected out into the objects of the space in which I lived—a lamp, a blanket, a tiled surface—and either I sank down in submission to the hold of this space upon me—or all of a sudden, usually late a night, I would rapidly slip back on my clothes and head out into the night in my car, rushing down the streets in search of the face, the hands, the laugh that might at last carry me away from myself.

I no longer believed in such a refuge—if I ever did. Yet the phantoms of hope can still transfix me for the whole night through as I stand and walk and pace, though not often sit, because if I sit I will fall asleep and thereby transform the city in which I live like a shadow into something other than what it is, burning away those spaces I inhabit, and all distance, and all separateness. I will awake: if only I could imagine this one thing—and then hold it there, firmly, without ever losing my grip. But how?

○

A manta of short dark hairs, slightly curled, embraces my chest: it peeps up out of the top of my T-shirts and open collars like tendrils reaching up. Yet I am always surprised, T-shirt finally off, to be aware again of the presence of the winged shape, a kind of brand which might, if I chose to read it thus, connect me with a race—as would the wash of slightly straighter hairs on the back of my hand that works its way up my forearm, stopping at the elbow. I am neatly haired, as if drawn or sketched with a fine pen, almost too animal-like for my own taste—as if my markings were those of some breed of domestic animal.

Nor was my surprise any less or greater this particular evening, or rather that clicking change of consciousness, a slight adjustment to the new reality of being much less clothed than an instant before, though I had been too lost in thought to have made the shift right away, of being almost but not quite naked, of being almost wholly revealed to the space and objects around me, and of that sensation of slight prickling as my skin (or so I presumed) accustomed itself to being bare to the damp yet warming air of the rooms.

I glanced down, ran a hand over stomach and chest, and thought once again of those somewhat peculiar-seeming markings on my body, and whose equivalents on others have so often fascinated me, and whose bearers I am drawn to in futile speculations. Or rather in the fascination of the endless composition of the catalog of body types I have assembled haphazardly in memory—those I have seen on the beach or in cafes and bars and even supermarkets, in that endless selection of—what?—perhaps perfect maleness I almost unwillingly seek—of perfect form at a certain age, in that time suspended just before the mature adult begins to show the effects of gravity or alcohol or fear or weariness and falls into the prolonged decay of middle age and becomes a parody of his younger self, and wears the clown face of one who remembers he was once young and beautiful and knows now his moment has passed—moment he too carelessly threw away at the time, thinking it would last forever, or at least last longer than that such short time.

I would not be one of those, I once again resolved: I would hold to my hour, knowing that at every minute it was about to end, and when my time passed, I would cling to it, and then would somehow transform myself into another kind of being.

I did not need to seek out my watch or the calendar on my cell phone. I knew I had between a few months and only a year at the most. And I knew now that I wouldn't readily perceive the change—except perhaps in the casual glances of others—of how, instead of drawing subtly near, in some sidelong manner, they would keep their distance and slip brightly away to another face. And I also knew that it could happen long before I would become aware of it. Which is to say that perhaps it already had.

O

I found myself pacing rapidly through such thoughts in order to warm myself, in the U-shaped course between bathroom, past the bed, through the living room and into the kitchen and back, circling tightly in the small spaces to make the turn. Within a few cycles I managed to warm myself with my modest exertions, to the point that the slightly cooler air of the rooms soon served to refresh me and I even took pleasure in veering close to the drafty back door, in the coolest recesses of the kitchen, and whose window shade I pulled down on perhaps the fifth pass. In time, the rooms heating up, and with perhaps even my walking passage through the space serving to mix warm and cold layers together, I began to smell the rising odor of perspiration which had broken through the now exhausted effects of my masking deodorant. Now and then a gust of wind struck the west wall, and the whole building creaked, and the glass ticked in the frames, and then there came the clatter of a garbage can lid in a neighboring carport followed by the hollow thumping of an empty cardboard box walking up the alley. And now and then I would pause before the glass front door and stare into the darkness toward the strip of ocean visible during the day between two buildings but at night usually not, except during a strong full moon, during an exceptionally clear night, which this was not. At most I could make out a sliver of the street lamp globe that stood on the seaward edge of the broad cement sea walk that ran along the beach for miles in both directions. I might, if I stood long enough, see the bobbing head of an evening stroller or runner who had decided to brave the wind. In this position I would be visible from a narrow stretch of the walkway that passed between alley and sea walk to someone looking at a certain angle, probably a rare event, even during bright crowded weekend days. The casual looker would have seen this evening the half-lit form of a skimpily clad man standing at a window, a not unusual occurrence in the neighborhood—where during the occasional hot nights of early autumn there are sometimes rashes of people flaunting their nudity, as in some kind of spontaneous carnival—by the young seeking, momentarily at least, to tear down the opaque walls they sense themselves imprisoned within—in order to proclaim—what?—an instant of animal solidarity.

I resumed my barefoot pacing, the breezes of my passage circulating between legs and arms, and flowing across my bare back; I could feel the seconds being paced away, the minutes, and eventually the hours.

O

Another lull came in the wind against the building and the distant surf, admitting again the faint, almost imperceptible throbbing of the city. I had paused in my pacings and stood near the center of the living room on the bare floor and was now holding back my breath, to make as little sound as possible. There comes a moment in my long evenings when sometimes I begin to feel it. Not always, or perhaps not even very frequently, even rarely, but those are the evenings that stand out, and so I tend to think of it as a far more common experience than the reality. Was this to be the one? A loud creaking in the floor, the slam of a car door downstairs, the cycling on of the refrigerator could all spook the moment. I waited.

Then, slowly, it began, a sensation of detachment or parting, as if the great machine of the city out there beyond the glass and screens of the windows was beginning to drift away toward some distant future while I now stood still in this space, more alone now as it grew slowly more distant—yet so large and churning that it would take days or months or even a lifetime for it to pass completely out of sight. It rumbled on without me in its dull roar now and then broken by faint wails and shrieks, while I stood breathless in a fragile contraption of space on top of the still earth. It was moving, crawling, buzzing, the distant excrescence, swarming mindlessly away, somewhere else, slow, glacial, toward some distant collision or collapse or sinking into the ocean— while I stood frozen in place, wondering whether the vibrations I felt, the trembling, in my feet were from its distant thundering or only the internal tensions of my own body.

The wind swung back and struck the building with a low rumble, and the surf answered in a long pounding crescendo. I wondered at that moment whether there might be other solitaries positioned evenly throughout this far-flung city and the others of the world, standing immobile in sparsely furnished rooms, deep in a kind of social coma, while everything else outside rushed headlong on from minute to minute—like rare owls requiring vast territories for their provisioning. Would we find each other in that moment when at last the restless tide of the city had withdrawn, leaving us perhaps just within sight of each other on the bare and quiet landscape? Would we be able to recognize each other?

○

The distance was short, no more than a hundred and fifty yards. I had traversed it hundreds or even thousands of times in reality, and mentally countless times more: down the redwood steps, past the garage, out into the alley, up the alley north to the cement sidewalk that passes through the mound of sand (which in heavy weather will wash and blow over the walkway) and then west between the two apartment buildings to the sea walk with its low cement wall and streetlamps and concrete benches every fifty yards or so, and during the day scatterings of strollers of all ages which give way late in the warm afternoons to clumps of high school kids in wet suits with surfboards—and at night to the occasional couple or desperate solitary pacing the interminable walk, or the jogger, when the tide is up or the night too dark to trust running at the edge of the surf. In the distance there might be shadowy figures around a bonfire in that strip where such things were still permitted, and shouts and laughter carrying over the dull roar of the surf, and the smell of wood smoke wafting through the air. Beyond midnight there was no one, unless the moon was full, and unless a late night party had spilled over on to the sand; but tonight was windy and moonless, and no one would be out, unless another who, like me, would seek the buffeting of the cold, damp wind, and trust the leaning thrustings of bare feet into the yielding sand, and then know the strange firm warmth of the damp packed sand and feel suddenly the foaming tongue of water washing up over bare feet.

I interrupted my circling to pause at the night stand and pick up my watch. It was not quite ten.

○

I would choose a high tide in winter because beyond a certain point quickly attained there could be no turning back, or rather would choose that moment an hour or so after the peak when the tide would be sweeping back out to sea. I could imagine the noise up close but not in the darkness, and my imaginings were always of a murky but visible darkness where I would be able to see, as in some illustration, miles to either side under the water—perhaps phosphorescing kelp beds, the hulk of a freighter known to lie off shore, the ruins of a collapsed pier, perhaps even schools of large silvery fish; but I could not imagine that I would see nothing, suddenly. It would have to be a slow and easeful thing, a kind of dimming, where the light became slowly softer, and sound ceased, and then touch, and then memory; and I would not even know that the taste of my slowly parting lips was that of salt.

I knew this to be an illusion—along with that other sensation of arms crooked at elbows as I would be embraced by the white foam of the breakers, like huge down comforters being flung about me, and which would surge up under my raising arms; and hip thrust forward, testicles withdrawing from the rush of cold water to hide like sensitive sea anemones, and the plunging roar overhead and into eyes and ears and nose—and the hissing bubbles of foam—and that swept off my feet I would be carried off in a spasm of brilliant cold and light, and would explode back into constituent elements of the universe.

These were the illusions I was fond of. It was clear that I still had a greater use for them than for what I guessed would be the reality—that I would be paralyzed by the coldness of those waters, their impenetrability, and at the vastness that licked at the edge of my fleck of existence.

○

I paused at the bowl.

The bowl is of pottery, glazed in a dark translucent cobalt blue, with the lines of its turning faintly visible through the glaze, and of a shape that flares out from the narrow base to nearly ten inches in diameter. In it I toss bits of paper I need to keep awhile: receipts, addresses, clippings, photos, the rare postcard or letter, with which the bowl becomes filled perhaps twice a year, before I go through it all to cull out what has become meaningless or irrelevant. It is the one place in my apartment the world outside can claim as a toehold, the one place a stranger might remark, having flicked through the contents of the bowl, "So you lead a normal life after all." And true, that might be a fair conclusion—that here is proof of all those little connections that must be woven together for even the most minimal of social existences, such as mine. Yet that existence floats more and more remotely from what I know to be my real life, a life that barely manifests in any public way—so much so, in fact, that I sometimes think of it going on without me, on its own trivial and self-effacing little ways, determined to be mildly pleasing to others, wanting even to be liked, wishing to slide unthreatened from minute to minute and from day to day. That other knows the words and gestures. He often surprises me at how well he walks through them, at even his degree of competence or even social intelligence. But he is not me. He is more like a child grown up and become unrecognizable by acquiring mildly offensive tastes and habits—but whose kinship I must now and then acknowledge. It is his clothes, not mine, that litter this place.

And I think of the glazed bowl as his, and I permit its presence among my possessions on a chest-high windowsill of the sort occasionally employed in the neighborhood for the collections of beachcombing artifacts—shells, floats, crab legs, scraps of fishnet and the like—only because I hardly ever see it, and I think of it as not there, except occasionally at such moments when I awake to the fact that it is something we possess in common; and I stand, looking across at it, a little below eye level, where it perches on the sill, reflection of itself in the glass, and my two dark eyes staring out of the blurred shadows of my face.

O

The booklet listing the tide tables for this section of the coast—not as accurate as the version to be found on the Web, but close enough, and it will have to do since I make a point of locking up laptop and tablet at work and never bringing them home—the tide table booklet peeped out at an angle above all the other scraps of paper in the bowl, and I reached up and fished it out with a little sawing motion meant to free it of its potentially clinging companions. I resumed pacing as I thumbed through it and read down the column to the evening's date, then across to the hour: 11:43. A little star that burst in the depths of my throat surprised me: a reprieve. But a short reprieve, not a long one of a day or even a week while the hour of the high tide worked toward some ideal late evening or early morning hour. Eleven forty-three: a perfect time, and soon.

Without being conscious of having crossed the room or of picking up my watch again, I found myself staring at its wide-flung hands, reading twenty past ten, over an hour before the moment of high tide.

I listened. The surf was muffled but insistent in its regular pounding, which sounded slightly sped up. It would probably seem to hold in position for the next hour or so before showing signs of withdrawing, and then soon, even at night, it would be clear to eye and ear that the retreat was in full flow.

○

The wind beat against the west side of the building. A spasm of trembling rippled across my skin, perhaps set off by a faint draft through the room, a brush of cool air across ankle and calf, like the entwining tail of a cat seeking a caress. Or so I first told myself, on realizing that I had been standing in one place for some minutes, after my darting movement to the night stand to look at the watch, and that my body had become rubbery with sleep and was now tingling with wakefulness again; and a flushed sense on my forehead told me my thoughts had released a quickening dose of adrenalin.

It would be cold, yet my path was a matter of less than five minutes, and I would be at a fever pitch of excitement and anticipation: the minutes would pass in a flash. And I reminded myself that I had deliberately chosen this kind of moment long ago (though the storm I could not have predicted) rather than a balmy autumn night, with the moon full and the water warm, and a sense of expectation hovering over the glowing scene—where my fleeting presence on the possibly crowded beach would be taken as some prank—and when I could not count on being alone—where there was too much chance of some encounter that would have lured me back from the edge of my impulse—that always unexpected collision of flesh to flesh, the underside of an arm, the unbalanced fumbling, and yet the pouring relief of distance closed, as if I had traveled a thousand miles on foot for that touch.

No, not thus. Such possibilities would be closed in the cold raging embrace, into which I would launch the useless perfection of whatever it is that I am, as crazed with fear at that final contact as I have ever been at the pawing thefts—which all touches conceal.

○

But I had slept or dozed. Beneath the surface of these calculations there was a flickering memory of wakening, and of some brief sweet hope immediately extinguished in this present. And then it came back to me that I had been thinking, off to the side of my mind, of the meadow to which I drive and hike several times a year in the warmer months, in the mountains to the north, a lozenge-shaped space set among the pine trees through which a small slow-moving steam meanders, and where I always go with the intention of never returning home. The place I seek is to the higher ground where I sunbathe with a view over the top of the tall grass of the meadow and its approaches, and I pass the day surveying the scene, working out the lines of sight, the protected hollows in the surrounding woods, watching the light change, the clouds, the birds skip through, and the insects hovering in columns above the little pools, where I take occasional dips to cool off, and where the arms and legs and torso of the strange creature I have brought here, this sad intruder, this self, become by the end of the day almost uncontrollably frenzied with delight in the dancing puzzle of heat and light and air and water.

Even out there, in the meadow, alone, I chatter to myself throughout the day, in my excitement of having reached it again and found it unchanged, to the point that by the time the sun begins dropping behind the tops of the pines I am almost shouting out loud to myself, even though I know I must soon leave, because I have not prepared myself for a night here, have brought little food—and because yet again I have failed to unclothe my-self from my chattering.

The sun dropped lower. Fingers of cool air began to feel their way into the hollow. I slipped back on my clothes and knew at last a moment of silence. The first thought that then came to me was that I would have no trouble at all in going through the verbal motions of paying for a tank of gas and a foil-wrapped snack warmed in a little oven, at some roadside store on the way back home.

○

I knew that though I could slip away in this way, to the meadow, or into the night somewhere, the surf, they—the others—in their infinite intelligence would sooner or later track my course and peel away my habits and reasonings—that in a sense they had already planned for this and had made allowances for it. I was or would become to them sooner or later another case or statistic, another dot, another magnetic impulse, another pixel, to serve their impassive reasoning and logic, because I had never been anything but those things, I had always been their file, their case, their spectator or consumer with this or that taste or habit, and their logic was so strong and persuasive that I had no choice but to be what was useful to them, including the illusion that it was really "a me" who decided these things, not them. I don't even know or care who they are, except I know they exist: I may even be, in my public self, one of them myself, or rather most surely I am one of them, which is to say that perhaps that is why I have so little curiosity about who they are. I can of course waken from this state and look around at the world and see it with again suddenly new and almost innocent eyes, and feel a sense of relief that after all perhaps they don't exist, and that perhaps I vaguely imagine them only as a kind of excuse, because perhaps I am the one who consents to their hypnotic powers. But then I begin to move about in the world again and I feel those forces and lines that pull me this way and that, as if I live a live on tracks, as guided by wires, or by imperceptible signals and waves, and I know that in some absent-minded and unfocused way I am being tracked and followed and listened to—it all seems so casual and even friendly—and I know I am lost again, even when I feel most free, behind the wheel, driving, taking the route that is twice as long as necessary to work and back, because here, even deep within the schools of bright metal fish, my little rebellion will be invisible to all but me—and that they control me, think my thoughts for me, and then reward me with my own desires and punish me with my own fears. They are there. I know because I take them to the meadow. And it is them that I will take to the sea.

○

My black low-rise briefs were of a brand that announced itself with a small rectangular label at about the protruding point of the left hip bone, sewn or glued on in some manner. I had at times thought of systematically going through my underwear and snipping off such labels, or blackening them with an indelible marker, thus to prevent them from following me, as it were, across the boundaries and on to the island of my privacy, where they intruded at such moments like the graffiti of hostile strangers.

There was also that business of the laundromat down the street where I washed and dried my clothes once every ten days or two weeks—and those moments when I must tumble out my wrinkled dirty clothes into the washer, and then fish them out thirty minutes later, all damp and twisted like entrails, and must cart them over to the dryer, to repeat the process. I am always disturbed to find a sock or handkerchief or a piece of flimsy underwear of either sex left behind in the drying before I put in my own clothes, and the thought of leaving behind so publicly a pair of my briefs fills me with as much alarm as leaving behind offerings of fingernail clippings, say, or snippets of hair. To mark them by blackening out the labels or cutting them off would make them too personally mine—and hold them back from the rescuing possibilities of anonymity. I have at lease once refused to retrieve from the turquoise green plastic basket of left-behind clothing a pair of gray briefs I knew indisputably to be mine, because in some manner I felt they had been soiled by a week of exposure to the curious hands of my unknown neighbors, under the humming array of fluorescent tubes. Finally they disappeared from the basket—and gave rise to the even more disturbing thought that someone else could have taken up wearing them. It was thus fortunate that I had not marked the labels, either the outside brand or the twin inside tags that noted size and washing instructions.

For weeks afterward I debated switching laundromats, and as also a way of lightening the demeaning burden of washing my own clothes in public—where intimate details of my life are or can be subject to the casual scrutiny of anyone at all—and where I am often too long in the company of those I feel are seeking a pretext to approach me.

My general trimness extends to restraint in the production of bodily effluvia, and as a result my clothing rarely emits more than the faintest odor of use or habitation, even after several days, unless the weather is unusually hot and humid; and I probably need to wash my clothes far less than I do. I wash them more out of suspicion than need, which enables me to enter the laundromat casually, even jauntily, as if in some way I am washing my clothes not because I so desperately need to—the case perhaps of my laundromat neighbors—but because in some manner it gives me pleasure to do so—almost as if I am doing this as a favor to someone else, voluntarily, freely, not out of need. In fact, to avoid any kind of last minute panic, I am always careful to do my laundry a good week before I completely run out of clothes, and I never wait or linger in the laundromat but immediately set off on a walk toward the beach timed to bring me back to the place the exact minute the cycle will complete itself. Also whenever possible I use the end machine in a somewhat cramped corner not favored by other patrons.

○

My intention had always been to do the laundry one last time the night before so as to leave behind no unwashed clothing at all, except what I had on that very night after coming home from work—less a matter of considering the sensitivities of whoever would enter my apartment to begin the task of dispersing my effects (as they will be called): landlord, acquaintance from work, police, even thief—than in deference to my own alarm at the thought of another person going through clothing that still bore the traces, the creases and wrinkles, of the presence of my body, to the point that I briefly debated whether I should cut socks and underwear into strips and flush them down the toilet or drop them into the public trash barrel on the sea walk on my way past. But such actions, if traced back and thought through, might seem pathological to some eyes, and cause the elaboration of pointless theories about what had happened and why, thereby subverting my intention of being as traceless as possible.

The laundromat was empty when I walked in, muslin bag tucked under arm, and in it, along with my laundry, a small pouch of detergent. I could count on the whole business of striding the length of the soap- and lint-scented space, past the huge portholes of the dryers, to my corner washer, of flipping open the lid of the yellow enameled machine, of dumping in my laundry, a small load because I thought I was ahead of my schedule— mistakenly, it soon turned out—of tearing open and emptying the plastic pouch, laying the quarters in the coin slots, setting the hot-cold switch, the wash-cycle knob—I could count on all this taking less than three minutes, giving me a good chance of getting out the door before anyone else might come in, of even being able to do both my washing and drying entirely alone for once, which could put me in a cheerful mood for days—however irrelevant that might be, this particular time.

But a scraping sound from the glass door, which often dragged on the jamb, announced that I was not to be alone. Nor were things going at all smoothly. My laundry uncharacteristically clung to the inside of the bag, or I had failed to open the drawstring fully, and in any case I had forgotten to remove the pouch of detergent first, and so had to rummage through the depths of the machine to fish it out. I had twisted myself around slightly to shield all this from the eyes of the new arrival, who was from the sounds of buttons brushing against metal stuffing laundry into a machine near the door.

Then I discovered that I had left my change at home. This was not like me. Every two weeks I pick up a roll of quarters at the bank so as to have a supply for parking meters, newspapers, and the laundromat, so as not to have to fumble through other denominations in my pockets—on the principle of economizing all gestures, or at least the small, draining ones. But how I had failed to transfer the change from the pocket of one pair of pants into the ones I had changed into left me bewildered: could I see, or did I only imagine, a pile of coins on the nightstand?

I looked up. A short and very slight young woman was bent over peering at the controls of the machine. There was something so uncomprehending in her unfocused stare or at the angle at which she held her head, or something about the stringiness of her hair, or the bundled up way her black sweater and perhaps woolen scarf were wrapped around her thin body—that I was pierced by a sense of her vulnerability. She was out of place in this robust neighborhood, like a refuge from a world in disintegration—or, I later was to think, the slumming child of wealthy parents.

There was a second scrape of the door, and in came an equally rumpled young man, thin and blond, in a dirty white shirt, who joined her at the machine. I could hear them murmuring to each other the instructions on the control panel.

It was then—more or less—I have lost track of the exact moment—but I think it was then that I broke into a cold sweat at the thought of being unable to go through with it for some stupid reason. I had anticipated that I would have doubts but was always able to push them away in the hope that they would not return, and of course not expecting they would ambush me at a moment like this of public weakness and confusion. I could see myself running barefoot back from the beach in the dark, down the walk, up the alley, quickly up the stairs, and back into the warm space of my apartment—I could see myself hastily dressing as if to clothe my uncontrollable shivering, not from the cold but from pushing so close to the edge, and then running back down the stairs and climbing into my car and driving out into the streets, for the relief of the speeding lights. I would be suddenly famished.

When I recovered myself they were gone, their machine contentedly chugging away. I tore the open end of the detergent pouch and dumped the contents into the receptacle. I had even forgotten my wallet. The only thing to do was walk back to the apartment, scoop up the change (wherever it was) and return. And then, back in the apartment, I was to discover yet one more thing, that I had brought only half my laundry to the laundromat, having pushed a pile of it out of sight behind the closet door. By now, angry at the collapse of my little plans, I left it there.

○

Left thumb behind the narrow elastic band, I slipped the briefs down my thighs and calves and, one foot stepping out, took them off the other raised foot, the right, and wadded them up and tossed them over toward the laundry bag just inside the closet. The cooler air of the room seemed momentarily to swirl around between my legs, and I peered down at the plum-colored knob and its companion sac nested in the short curly black hairs, and I could feel it beginning to unfurl and stretch as if pushing out to seek the now absent confinement.

I resumed pacing. My body was at last free from all its bindings and fetters, and all the messages they carried to me and pressed against my skin, and wearing at it and chafing it all day long—a kind of flexible body cast echoed also in the loose fitting seat of the car or the padded chairs at work, even the building which I entered and stayed inside for hours at a time: clothing too, meant to press and bind me into a certain form, to ends nobody could guess—other than that I must always be pressed and held into some form or other, in what I wrapped around myself, and the shape in which my thoughts were to be housed.

I was free to roam my island again, after a long and careful voyage through the day and night—I had landed again and could now pace jauntily back and forth across the bare oak floor, the beach of my apartment, again be the creature unrecognizably remote from its public self—without telltale trappings other, perhaps, than the cut of my hair, and in the way I walked or held my arms, or how straight or slouched I trod, or in the fading marks left by elastic at waist or above ankles. But even now, the reptile skin of society sloughed off, now fully incarnated again, I knew there would be something new and unrecognizable in my bearing—and certain gestures or ways of looking, a shift in the eyes, a way of tossing back the head, a freer drop in the hips, a springier tread as I walked—that I alone could feel, not observe in any distant way. It was a truly youthful self that moved through the dimly lit rooms, stripped of all those marks and cramped habits of movement that were not yet visible to others but probably soon would be in a year or two, in time, as they filled themselves out and became more pronounced: the way soon I would not want to be.

It was this body, this self, this youth, I would almost say, that lived without past and without future, in the always glorious moment, at the moment of perfect ripeness or within close memory of it—a being that pushed away all else except the beats of a pounding heart and the tingling of unconstrained extremities—and denied all origins and all destinations, all clothings of the mind that twist and distort and imprison all in the webs of the human.

But they seemed now distant, those long burning moments when, member erect, all of existence became sexualized, moments that flowed in unbearable waves and impelled me far and wide, as if to find some physical limit, some end to my desire—and then withdrew, leaving me small and disappointed, and more alone than before, and I would return exhausted from my always failed quest, and quietly push closed the car door behind me. And now, uncertainly tumescent, unwilling to flood to erection, it bounced as I paced: ignore it, I told myself, pay no attention to it—that creature whose animal existence would lead me back to the dream of easy comforts, fleeting ecstasies, the crowd, the world.

I had broken free again tonight, as I had almost every night, in this slow dance in which I peel away the work of the days—only tonight I wondered if I would finally take the last step. Were the doubts finally stilled? Had I finally wearied my fears into submission? They were there, but weakened and exhausted, and not believable in their claims of certainty, at this moment when I knew at last the unarguable fact: that of this act nothing that stepped beyond the routine could be guessed in advance—that up to a certain point it was only a walk to the edge of the surf, like any other, like countless others.

Tonight I would dispatch yet another self into oblivion—as I have done countless times—to awake transformed into another, by a miraculous dream. I would awake somehow, somewhere, sticky with its explosion, and find myself again strapped into hope and chattiness, the blade of grass that forces its waving slip into the air amid the endless concrete; I would awake to find myself living in a herd, a flock, like an animal, indistinguishable from the others, alive by the day, in the moment, without history, without future, no longer the solitary creature bereft of his herd, no longer held apart by the bright pincers of his intelligence, mercilessly commanded to live alone among things, in the endless cities of things. Tonight I would dispossess myself of yet another self, another impersonation. The waves—or sleep—would do it. Which?

My nakedness would be my authority that would both propel me on and turn away all those who, guessing an intention, would hesitate—because I would have no clothes to which they might speak, only the starkness of bare flesh.

I could entertain fears, as I paced within the apartment, of being surreptitiously observed—but not out of shame, rather from a fear of a kind of possession—of stealing glimpses of me in this state without my consent, to prurient ends I could readily imagine—or to some end not my own. But to step outdoors thus, into the windy night, with always the risk of encountering late-night strollers or carousers, was another matter, because it was I who was offering myself up—as an example, a vision, of the ultimate evasion from the grooves and blinds and wires.

I hoped, I told myself, for no witnesses, for a clean, unobserved slipping away, with the pounding waves closing overhead, in the darkness, or so I told myself to hope.

Yet I knew—as I paced—that in this last matter I wondered whether I was—perhaps at last—not being honest with myself—and that perhaps I secretly craved or treasured an expectation of someone out strolling, who would turn at that last moment—too far out—too late—someone from out of town, leaving early the next morning, who knew no one, and who would be haunted the rest of his life by that brief ambiguous vision.

Yet I knew who was sending that message: the other self, the public self, who dresses this body in the morning and who inserts it into car and street and city, who clings to the last minute hope of being able to release in me, at the edge, the infections of memory; and who attempts to flood me with other times and other days, and who will then raise all the impossible hopes—and I will stand there being racked with all that I have again and again denied—to free myself—shivering in the cold.

But I mock him. I mock him as he stands there on the concrete walkway, the grit of damp sand beneath bare feet, in the wind, and the drops of a warm rain splattering across his naked body, under the street lamp. I mock his shivering, his sobbing, hunched over, hands cupping his balls, waiting for someone to come with a rough woolen blanket and lead him away. Will he enjoy the ride? What will the greasy plastic seat feel like under bare thighs? Will he answer the questions, will he say that he is from such and such a place, born here or there, of these or those? Will he give his age? Profession? Will he divulge the names of others? Through clenched chattering teeth will he mutter, will you please send someone to my apartment, to get some clothes?

The dresser in the bedroom. Will he explain? I'll pay whatever is charged. Will he ask: Please?

○

Something in the wind or in the changes of barometric pressure now and then caused an odor to diffuse out into the kitchen from the cupboard or the unused oven, perhaps even from some vent, an odor of old cooking or baking grown not quite stale; and it was the reappearance of this smell that brought my pacings, which had grown precipitous and loud, to an abrupt halt at the threshold of the kitchen.

I stood testing the smell. Something perhaps like bread or yeast, though not quite a bakery smell, or perhaps of a vegetable soup, and in those few instants when it would remain fresh in my nostrils before sniffing would render nerve endings insensitive to it, I wondered whether I should walk slowly to the far end of the apartment, pause there for awhile before returning, nostrils refreshed, to inhale the fleeting vapor, which was probably generated by nothing more than the grime in the depths of the oven or broiler and even joints in the linoleum—the last traces perhaps of a woman who had lived here before and who had spent her evenings or weekends cooking for friends—or the ghosts of past meals, which my own lack of kitchen activity had done nothing to dispel.

The bath often exhaled another odor at the same time, of a sweetish soap yet of no one brand, or of shampoo or toothpaste, from probably the whitish grime around the base of the shower stall and bath tub, from perhaps even the drains, but tonight it remained quiescent or was over-ridden by the slight smell of mold, which meant that the shower curtain needed to be washed again.

I stood on the threshold of the bathroom pondering these occasional presences which had the odd effect at times of turning this most private space into something very public, and which could oppress me with the weight of a collective presence; and I could see with sudden clarity that my solitude was a carefully cultivated and studied condition, fastidiously maintained by a system of both denials and assenting gestures—any one of which I could, at any minute, with no effort at all, simply lift.

And instead of these presences this time intruding on me, I almost welcomed them—or already, the memory of them, they were so fleeting—as distractions, as guests, which I never invite into my space, who might somehow say the few words which might turn me back.

I stood alert, motionless, almost not breathing, eyes half closed, listening. Near the living room door, the floor creaked: a board expanding in the rising humidity. Then, from within the depths of the shower stall, the loud splat of a drip hitting the fiberglass floor of the stall from a drop of six feet. I reached in and tightened the valve.

○

Of course I might have lived my life in some other way—that instead of sealing myself off in a hermetical chamber of calculation and measurement of the optimum distance from infections and toxins, from the disease of life itself, I could have learned the forms of abandon, could have mastered those emotions I saw others walking through so easily—I could have put aside those endless calculations of distance and closeness, did not my own sun within burn so brightly, radiating only outward. No one I knew could I admire, and I refused to admire anyone I could not know, none of the phantom gods, which left only the one self, unapproachable from without in the heat of its burning stare which so easily disproved those others of themselves.

And what finally will be the difference between striding into the waves alone with only the trivia of the day—than if I were to do so with a heavy suitcase of what they call fine memories? As the lighter traveler my passage will be easier and more trouble-free, with perhaps less pain and no grief, no clinging to a past I killed off long ago—with nothing left but odors from an old stove, a bathtub, from apparitions I can no longer visualize, ghosts sensed in the expressions and gestures of strangers. I let my past die first, rather than the other way around, in which my present, my presence, dies, but past flickers on. My afterlife will be a garage sale or flea market stall, half a weekend at most, and then I will be dispersed—a few small kitchen appliances, some bedding and towels, some mostly clean clothes, a few dirty ones, some bills to be paid against a healthy bank balance. If I have a ghost, it will be a brief one, a faint somewhat fresh odor wafting briefly out of a thrift shop clothes rack.

It will be my way of becoming an ordinary person.

○

I picked up my watch and carried it over to the electric baseboard register along the north wall, where I stood with my back to it, warm air brushing up over my legs and buttocks before dispersing itself at my lower back. I studied the sweep second hand of the watch, its little jerks from second mark to second mark, or not quite, as the hand never exactly lined up with the mark, being off by a fourth or third of an increment. Was this a defect?

It was almost midnight. The moment of high tide was ten minutes ago, and soon the waves would be in retreat. I could hear no change in their pounding, and the wind still buffeted against the stucco wall to my back. From where I stood I could see at an angle from the glass door a triangular strip of the walkway and a street lamp, and the blackness beyond. The warm current of air from the heater carried the odor of perspiration up, and I was startled by the coldness of a downward trail made by a bead of sweat below my left armpit. I flinched.

From now on I could go. Any time from this very moment to three or four hours from now, even later, though the longer I waited the more I would be seeking to renegotiate or evade the original terms of the intention—which in clear-headed moments had its compelling rationale. I would grow tired and querulous with myself the longer I waited, and would begin to demand exceptions, would question my own reasoning—and I could see myself falling into bed in confusion at four in the morning, yet one more time. How often had I done this?

I had not thought about the key. Should I leave the door locked or unlocked? To leave it open or unlocked would to a degree say that from now on this apartment was no longer mine or necessarily mine, and would be to release this space, these four rooms, to some other fate. To lock the door, as it was now locked, would be to still claim possession, even later, beyond, though it would not prevent me from returning: there was a spare key around the back side of the rusty black cap of the porch lamp housing. But I knew this was all some kind of sophistry. When I went out the door, if I went out the door, I would rely on the instinct of my fingers to do whatever they would with the inside button latch. They would have to take care of it one way or another.

○

The apartment stank, I was certain, of all my breathing and evaporations over the past hours: I could imagine but not sense the stench that would greet me on my return after, say, a quick trip downstairs for something left in the car, or for the neglected mail, which I no longer had any interest in; it would, on re-entry, embrace me as a sweetish, cloying smell, these gases of combustion and decay.

The apartment was so tightly built that only occasionally would the counter-scent of the waves break through this other unsensed odor, but the pounding of the breakers came like a giant irregular heartbeat through the windows and walls and even, when I stood still and managed to quiet my own tremblings, up through the floor, up through my bare soles moistly adhering to the varnished oak boards the color of honey.

From where I stood, back to heater, storing up the flow of heat, I could see my jeans tossed on the bed and the shadowy shapes of underwear, shirt, socks just inside the closet door, and top of the dresser my ring and change, bits of myself I had shed over the past several hours. But this evening as never before I felt a certain sadness at the sight, and even affection for the rumpled forms, and at the games and rituals and habits they embodied, to me at least—a coded map of a life I had decided to abandon—and I could even read in their folds an invitation to smooth them out and re-fill them with the shapes of this body, to regain that now former life, to continue on with its incomprehensible patterns that seemed to lead nowhere but to a wearing down to a state of bland exhaustion and indifference, in preparation for the slaughter.

Oh yes. I had thought of therapies and help, but to what end? To reconcile me to a life in which I was to feel good about this self in a doomed world? To end the delusions of this self by casting them into the delusions of some amorphous collectivity that has discovered the secret of—what?—health?

This was it: a sparsely furnished apartment, a prison, where late at night a naked man stood before a heater, with two choices: the waves, which would break and pulp and liquefy him into their turbulent universe, back down into the compounds and elements that perhaps would be reconstituted or equally might never be reconstituted into something else, some lump of matter, some creature, some flow, forever; or else to resume the body case of clothing and perform again the mechanical rituals that defined him as an over-specialized member of a species which now combed the earth bereft of purpose, if ever there had been one.

I pondered the symmetries, knowing that in my state of heightened fatigue and anticipation—my legs ached at the back of the thighs during such moments—further elaboration might well render them false or, worse, that I would become pleasantly bewildered once again at the complexity of these spinnings. This was the moment. With no more hesitation I stepped toward the door.

O

I pulled the door closed. The cold damp wind enfolded me. The doormat prickled under my bare soles. The electrical lines up and down the alley swung ponderously on their insulators, and the orange street lamps rocked back and forth on brackets. There was a steady rain of sand blown against some metal object down below in the darkness. I thought: I am going to my wilderness.

I padded down the wooden stairs, on to the concrete apron of the garage, and slipped past the crouched form of my car and then out into the alley, which appeared deserted. The cold had already numbed my skin, yet I could still feel the planes of my body giving form to the wind's caresses as I set off in a slow jogging run up the alley north, toward the walkway that led to the water. I was momentarily possessed by a nagging fear that barefoot I would tread on a piece of broken glass or jagged metal in the dark. I chided myself for not having thought ahead. Nothing would have been lost wearing thongs or even running shoes, nothing at all. Yet I was simultaneously swept by a rush of exhilaration at how easy everything was.

In the distance a car backed out of a garage or parking space but turned and headed the other way, its red tail lights flashing momentarily brighter as it paused at a cross street, before vanishing to the right, inland. I turned west on the walkway, which shortly vanished into a smooth parabola of sand heaped up by the wind and through which I stepped carefully, almost tip-toeing. Though cold, the sand offered the warmth of protection to my feet, almost up to the ankles.

At the corner of the stucco apartment buildings I glanced back. I had left lights on all over the apartment, which conveyed the impression of a late night emergency. My neighbor's windows were dark except for the glow of a night light or small computer screen through a north facing window, probably the bedroom.

A ragged wind whipped across the sea walk from the direction of the surf. I could taste salt on my lips and could feel—or imagine the feeling of the slightly sticky, slightly abrasive coating spreading across my skin and stiffening my hair. The street lamps cast a weak glow out across the beach and illuminated the tops of the breakers as they rose in an oddly muffled way—as if consumed by their own curtains of collapsing water. The breakers seemed further out than I had imagined. Had I misread the tide tables?

There was an opening in the seawall, and steps down to the sand, just under the nearest streetlamp, and I trod down their gritty risers into the sand, which was damp but not wet. A form in a tattered sleeping bag, right up against the black boulders that served to protect the sea walk, did not stir as I passed. The sand felt warm against my feet. I was surprised the waves had not sent running tongues of foam up this far. The peering lights of the apartments lining the sea walk projected faint shadows ahead of me, of blurred shapes staggering in unison across the sand. Then the sand firmed and grew warmer, and I could hear the hiss of the bursting bubbles of the breakers' wide-flung aprons of water.

The beach was wider and more open that I had expected. Perhaps the storm, its changes of pressure, had altered the tide, even diminished its effect. I had spent the evening imagining the surf to be more ferocious than it was.

The sand grew damper and softer and warmer under my tread: I would be following in the wake of a withdrawing wave. Abruptly in the darkness my feet stubbed into the hissing, foaming water, which rose to my calves, water at first stingingly cold and then almost warm, warmer than the wind.

I would have to wade, I realized, far out to the breakers, which seemed to have receded as fast as I had approached. I could remember in a fleeting, jumbled way, all the plans and exacting preparations that had led me up to this moment again and again, but then seemed as remote as the spray of lights that fanned out to sea at my back, lights and windows that peered day after day, night after night, for something that would never appear. Only my clothes seemed close, almost within reach, still imbued with the warmth of my body, strewn around the bedroom and in the closet.

I thought: this is my wilderness: I have entered into it.

I stood there for a moment, water rising and falling around my ankles. This was when the trembling began, a racking shaking of my whole form.

The wind dropped and my shivering ceased as abruptly as it had begun. In that instant of quiet, I could hear a joint creak, the sound of my own sharp, quick breathing, and the slow pounding of my heart.